The Sanibel Sunset Detective Goes to London

Also by Ron Base

Fiction

Matinee Idol
Foreign Object
Splendido
Magic Man
The Strange
The Sanibel Sunset Detective
The Sanibel Sunset Detective Returns
Another Sanibel Sunset Detective
The Two Sanibel Sunset Detectives
The Hound of the Sanibel Sunset Detective
The Confidence Man
The Escarpment
Heart of the Sanibel Sunset Detective

Non-fiction

*The Movies of the Eighties (*with David Haslam*)*
If the Other Guy Isn't Jack Nicholson, I've Got the Part
Marquee Guide to Movies on Video
*Cuba Portrait of an Island (*with Donald Nausbaum*)*

www.ronbase.com
Read Ron's blog at
www.ronbase.wordpress.com
Contact at
ronbase@ronbase.com

The Sanibel Sunset Detective Goes to London

RON BASE

Copyright © 2016 Ron Base

ISBN 978-0-9940645-1-6

*Publisher's Note: This is a work of fiction. Names, characters, places,
and incidents either are products of the author's imagination or
are used fictitiously. Any resemblance to actual persons, events, or
locales is entirely coincidental.*

West-End Books
133 Mill St.
Milton, Ontario
L9T 1S1

Text design: Ric Base
Electronic formatting: Ric Base

1

A bicycle rider discovered the body in the bushes near a pathway winding through Meanwhile Gardens. The path led to the Grand Union Canal behind Trellick Tower where Tree Callister and his wife, Freddie Stayner, had taken an apartment.

The apartment Tree and Freddie would occupy for a month was on the twenty-seventh floor of a building that, depending on your view, was either a grim, Stalinist-era monstrosity or an art deco masterpiece imprisoned in a German expressionist nightmare by Fritz Lang.

Tree thought he and Freddie were moving into Notting Hill, but, as he usually was when it came to geography, he was wrong.

Trellick Tower was actually located in the Royal Borough of Kensington and Chelsea, a couple of blocks north of Portobello Road with its traditional market. Like most things in London, the building came with history. Its design rose out of the imagination of the Hungarian architect Ernő Goldfinger—and yes, Tree had already learned that author Ian Fleming got into a discussion with Goldfinger's cousin on a golf course and then titled his next novel, *Goldfinger*.

Freddie's brother, Hale, had found the apartment for them. It featured sliding glass doors opening onto a balcony and a stunning view of London. Freddie was already in love with it, particularly since the single bedroom was dominated by a queen-size Hastens, one of the most expensive beds on the market, not to mention one of the most comfortable.

Tree and Freddie had come to London to attend the wedding of Freddie's nephew, Derek Stayner. Freddie had not seen Derek since he was a child, and Tree had never met him, but Hale, a retired American investment banker living in Golders Green, wanted the whole family together for Derek's marriage to—well, whomever Derek was marrying. Who was Derek marrying? Good question. Nobody seemed to know much about her. There was a name, Katrina Phillips, but not much more than that. Hale said she was beautiful. She worked in London, but doing what precisely wasn't known. A mystery woman was the way Hale summed her up over the phone. He didn't sound very happy about it. A mystery woman loved by Derek. "Whatever love is," Hale added.

"Now Hale," Freddie said. "That's no way to talk."

"It is the talk of a man who has been through the mill three times, and is exhausted by the experience, never mind a whole lot poorer."

"Tree's been married four times, and he's not cynical," Freddie said.

"He's probably lying," replied Hale. "Besides, in the end, he got you. Goodness knows how he managed that being—well, what is he? Some sort of detective on an island off the west coast of Florida? What's that all about? Under the circumstances, I would say he may not be cynical, but he is damned lucky."

"A body has been found in the area," the officer said.

"In the park," Freddie said.

Both police officers stiffened. "Yes, how did you know that?"

"We saw the police and emergency vehicles from our apartment," Freddie said.

"Did you see anything else, anything at all out of the ordinary?"

"I'm afraid not. We've only just arrived from America."

"Then we won't keep you. Thanks for your time."

"The body you found," Freddie said. "Is it a man or a woman?"

The older police officer hesitated before she said, "The victim is male."

"I'm so sorry," Freddie said.

The officers nodded, wished them a good day, and went off. Tree saw the blue London taxi coming to a stop at the curb. "That must be our ride," he said.

3

Hale Stayner's white-washed Tudor-style house on Corringham Road was mostly hidden behind the tallest hedge in the neighborhood. A stone walkway, flanked by a garden choked with hydrangeas, led to the entrance.

As Freddie and Tree approached, the front door opened to reveal Hale, tall, athletic-looking, intelligent blue eyes that seemed able to assess a situation in a moment, helpful in the banking business, Tree imagined. He wore the type of hounds tooth jacket that might be expected of the well-to-do Englishman about to entertain weekend guests. Or, possibly more accurately, an American doing a pretty good impression of an English country gentleman, not quite a gentleman and nowhere near the country.

Breaking out a big smile, showing off teeth of a whiteness that could only have been created in a dentist's office, Hale took Freddie in his arms for a bear hug and kisses on both cheeks. Then there was a hug for Tree. No kisses on the cheeks, though. "So good to see you both," he said. "Freddie, you never age, quite remarkable."

"London looks good on you, Hale," Freddie said. "I always expect you to produce a riding crop and ride to the hounds."

"Tree is a very good detective," Freddie said. "Too good, in fact. I'm hoping that bringing him to London means he stays out of trouble for the next month or so."

"Then get here my dear sister," Hale said. "We will figure all this out then."

And so they had come.

"Hurry and get dressed," Freddie said. "Hale is sending a car around so that we can have lunch together at his house. You're far too engrossed in these London tabloids."

Tree sighed and put his copy of *The Sun* to one side. "There's a report today about a member of the House of Lords videotaped snorting coke and cavorting with a couple of prostitutes. Lord Justin Butler. They call him Bad Butler. He's had to resign. The London political world is in an uproar. In the U.S. most politicians only do dull things like misuse tax payer money. They are much more interesting here."

"You're a voyeur," Freddie said.

"Politicians and prostitutes," Tree said. "Who can resist?"

"I hate to sound like a prude, but I can certainly resist," Freddie said. "What's more, I'm going to leave you here if you don't hurry."

"I don't think Hale likes me," Tree said.

"That's not true," Freddie said. "I couldn't resist you. How could he?"

"He doesn't think I'm rich enough for you."

"You're not rich at all," Freddie said with a grin.

"You married a poor, underpaid Chicago newspaper reporter," Tree said.

"Who promptly lost his job, moved to Sanibel Island, became a detective and got himself shot—twice."

"No wonder Hale doesn't like me," Tree said.

"Get dressed," Freddie replied, "before I shoot you."

2

"What's that going on down there?" Freddie said as Tree used the two separate keys required to lock the door to their apartment. She was peering out the windows that ran the length of the passageway.

"Going on where?" Tree finished locking the door.

"Down by the canal."

Tree followed her pointed finger. Sure enough, far below tiny figures darted around police and emergency vehicles. More tiny figures moved back and forth along the Grand Union Canal. It was a scene with which Tree was all too familiar in North America, a scene he never imagined he would have to witness in stately, law-abiding London. Tree liked to think the citizens here behaved themselves, except in British TV police dramas. Invariably those dramas presented middle-aged police inspectors who were always polite and solved the crime by finding the flaw in the timeline that led to the clue that identified the killer. All very genteel.

Nothing at all like rough, tough, gun-crazy Florida crime.

They went through the fire doors into a blue-tiled foyer. A sign beside the elevators warned that the miscreant who had been spitting on the floor had now been identified via recently-installed CCTV security cameras. Thus if he knew what was good for him, he had better stop spitting on the floor.

"You have been warned," Freddie said.

"I will try to do better," Tree said.

The elevator doors opened and a politely disembodied English voice announced, "The doors are opening."

"In case you didn't know," Freddie said.

Tree said, "These are my kind of people. I need all the help I can get."

"Doors are closing," the voice said.

And, sure enough, they were.

"What time are we supposed to meet Hale?" Tree asked when they reached the ground floor lobby.

"As soon as we can get there. His housekeeper has prepared a lunch."

"I'm impressed," Tree said, "although where your brother is concerned, I'm not surprised. It's sort of his style, isn't it?"

"Hale has too much money," Freddie said.

"In London, I don't think it's possible to have too much money," Tree said.

When they came out onto Golborne Road there was no car waiting, but there were two female London police officers in yellow vests.

The older of the two women stepped forward and said, "Excuse me, do you have a moment?"

Tree and Freddie came to a stop.

"We're making inquiries in the neighborhood," the older police officer continued. "I wonder if we might ask you a couple of questions."

"Yes, of course," Freddie said. "What's happened?"

"No hounds in Golders Green, I'm afraid. Locals wouldn't tolerate such barbarity."

He then inspected Tree. "As for you, Tree. Well, I suppose you do your best, don't you?"

"I struggle," Tree said. "But you look good, Hale."

"You're joking, of course. Between women and kids, I've aged a hundred years in the last year or so. I've had to give up cigars. Most booze. Life is grim, let me tell you, and it costs a fortune. Come in. Come in." He ushered them inside and closed the door.

They passed through an entry hall, walls filled with paintings, a staircase rising toward the second floor, and entered a blue sitting room with matching blue sofas. More oils that looked as though they might be worth something covered the walls. Over an impressive fireplace, partially blocked by a large urn with fresh flowers, a portrait in oils of a group of men in rich shades of brown and black engrossed in cards. To the right of the fireplace, big windows looked into what the British called a garden, while Americans, in their vulgar way, insisted was a backyard.

"I hope you both like salade niçoise. Emma my housekeeper does a superb salade niçoise."

"You're in luck, Hale," Freddie said. "We both like salade niçoise."

"The saints be praised," Hale said. "Come, sit down. Make yourselves at home. Can I get you a drink before lunch?"

Freddie wanted a glass of chardonnay. Hale frowned when Tree asked for sparkling water.

"That's right. You don't drink do you? They're liable to start throwing you out of restaurants over here, better be careful. They tend not to trust fellows who don't drink."

"I thought you said you weren't drinking, Hale."

"I said I had to give up *most* booze," Hale corrected. "I never said anything about *all* booze, *every* day."

Hale disappeared into the kitchen and was back a moment later with an open bottle of French chardonnay. He poured wine into a glass and brought it to Freddie. Then he was at a drinks cart, gleaming with liquor bottles crowded together so that there was barely room for the ice bucket from which Hale was now using a pair of silver tongs to pluck out an ice cube and drop it into a tall glass. He tipped the contents of a small Perrier bottle into the glass and handed it to Tree. Hale then half-filled a tumbler with Oban scotch, failing, Tree noticed, to add either ice or water. Today was the day Hale was drinking.

They settled onto the sofas. Hale took a deep swallow from his scotch and the color rose in his face. They chatted about this and that, the weather this summer, cool, and sunny with a little typical London rain thrown in for good measure.

Tree said he had visited the city often in the 1970s and 1980s when he was a reporter, but had never spent enough time here. "I'm looking forward to getting to know the city better in the next month," Tree said.

"Good luck with that," Hale said, making a face. "I barely know the place any more. London's changed so much. Everybody's tearing something down so they can replace it with places only oil sheiks from Dubai can afford, and even they're beginning to shake their heads.

"We're swamped with immigrants. You get on the tube these days and you never hear English spoken. The area around Paddington and Edgware Road, you'd think you were in another country."

"I love it," Freddie chimed in. "Where we are, it's very diverse and that makes it lively and fun, and certainly much different from Sanibel Island."

Hale made another face and said, "Yes, well, you always were the cheerful optimist about everything Freddie. What makes you so lovable, I suppose."

They talked of West End shows. Tree and Freddie had tickets for *The Curious Incident of the Dog in the Night-Time*, and were looking forward to it. Hale felt that, like just about everything else in London, the theatre scene had fallen on hard times. "American juke box musicals," he said disdainfully. "Why there's even something in the West End featuring the music of Michael Jackson."

"Can you imagine!" said Freddie in mock horror.

"Juke box musicals, and politicians cavorting with prostitutes. For the life of me, I really don't know what is happening to this country."

"That would be the Bad Butler," Tree said.

"So you've been reading about him." Hale made a face.

"Tree is obsessed," Freddie stated.

"Not obsessed," Tree protested. "Interested."

"Not that I have anything against cavorting around with ladies of dubious reputation, as long as you don't end up on the front pages of the tabloids. But then nothing is secret any longer, is it? Everyone gets caught doing everything. Very sad."

Hale finished his scotch and went into the kitchen emerging a few moments later with the salade niçoise his housekeeper had prepared. The table in the dining room had already been set. Tree and Freddie sat on either side while Hale served them and then poured more wine for his sister. He retrieved a large wine glass from the kitchen accompanied by what he said was a very good bottle of merlot, and poured himself a full glass. More evidence to Tree that what Hale said about his drinking, and what Hale actually did about his drinking, were two very different things.

"Look, I was going hold off until we finished with lunch," Hale said, following the usual exclamations from Freddie and Tree complimenting the fine quality of the food. "But damnit, I can't wait."

"Uh, oh," Freddie said, perhaps sensing the arrival of the storm clouds that inevitably swirled around her brother. 'Wait for what?"

"I'll get right to the point. I'm worried about this wedding," Hale said. "I don't like what's going on."

"What is going on, Hale?" Freddie asked.

"That's the problem in a nutshell. I don't *know*." He focused on Tree. "Here's my dilemma, Tree. I'm concerned about Derek, my son by my first wife. I must confess, what with one thing and another, I wasn't the most attentive father. Did my best with the boy, but he was mostly raised by his mother who spoiled him."

"Jill didn't spoil him," Freddie interjected.

"Your opinion, not mine, Freddie," Hale said. "In any event, he's had his ups and downs; a bit of trouble with drugs as a teenager that sort of thing. I suppose he's straightened himself around, but he is about to marry this Katrina Phillips, and like I told Freddie on the phone, I have no idea who she is or what she does. It's driving me crazy."

"Why don't you ask Derek?" Freddie said. "Or better yet, talk to Katrina herself."

"Derek won't talk about any of this. Says it doesn't matter. I'm interfering in his personal life. God knows how he would react if I went to Katrina. And who knows what she would have to say for herself."

"But presumably Derek knows what he has to know, and that's what counts," Freddie said.

Hale grimaced. "Derek appears to be blinded by this silly thing he insists on calling love."

"Imagine that," Freddie said.

"Yes, yes, love is all well and good, but one must also be pragmatic. Derek at some point will inherit a great deal of money. I want to make certain that the woman he marries is not taking advantage."

"Do you believe this Katrina Phillips is taking advantage?" Tree asked.

"I certainly have my suspicions, particularly when there seems to be so little information about her."

"I'm sorry you're feeling this way," Freddie said, sounding more impatient with her brother than sympathetic. "But at this point there doesn't seem to be much you can do about the situation does there? After all, the wedding is next week. I presume all the arrangements have been made."

"There's the thing," Hale said. "With Tree here, I think there *is* something that can be done."

"Me?" Tree looked at Hale in bewilderment. "What can I do?"

"Look, there are still five days to the wedding. You're a detective, Tree. You can poke around and make sure this young woman is legitimate. If you find nothing, all well and good. The couple lives happily ever after, I suppose. But if there is something—and I have a sneaking suspicion there is—then we could be helping my son avoid the biggest mistake of his life."

"We all make mistakes," Tree said. "But we have to make them ourselves, and hopefully learn from them. Besides, I am the wrong person to be doing this."

"What do you mean?" countered Hale. "You work as a private investigator in America, do you not? From what Freddie tells me you're practically a local hero back on Sanibel."

"Hero is not the word most people use," Tree said.

"But you've been involved in big cases. Murders. They've done media stories on you and your exploits. Tree, you're not just the man for the job, at this juncture, you are the *only* man."

Tree wanted to tell Hale that whatever he thought, whatever he had read, his bona fides as any kind of investigator were suspect. He had failed to solve much of anything over the course of his so-called career in private investigation. He had stumbled through most of the cases in which he was involved, surprised he had gotten out alive, let alone "solved" a case in any traditional sense.

"Tree's a much better detective than he gives himself credit for," Freddie chimed in, coming to his defense. "But he's a fish out of water in London. He doesn't know the lay of the land, isn't familiar with the people. Even if he was to do such a ridiculous thing as you're suggesting, I don't think he would be much help."

Freddie turned to Tree. "And you would never agree to anything like Hale is suggesting, would you, Tree?"

"No, no," Tree said quickly. "Of course not. I'm the wrong man for the job."

Hale rose from his chair, went to a sideboard and returned with an envelope. He sat at the table and took out photos which he spread in front of Freddie and Tree. "This is the young woman in question," Hale said, as though presenting evidence of a crime. "These were taken last year when Derek introduced me to his prospective bride."

The photographs showed Derek smiling happily into the camera, the light glinting off his eyeglasses, his arm around a stunning young woman. Katrina Phillips wore a black shirt open at the throat. She looked less happy and less certain than her fiancé.

Another photo: Katrina alone on a sofa, holding a glass of wine, looking away, caught unawares, long, long legs extended from a short skirt. He thought of a line from his days as a reader of pulp fiction detective stories: "Only the floor stopped her legs going on forever."

"She's lovely," Freddie said, stating the obvious.

Yes, she is, Tree thought. Skin, pale perfection, narrow cheekbones, softly lit, setting off wideset eyes containing a hint, Tree imagined, of darkness, everything framed by a shiny swatch of hair tumbling to her shoulders. You could fall in love with a face like that, and presumably that's what Derek had done.

'What do you think?" Hale was looking directly at Tree.

"I agree with my wife," Tree said carefully. "She's quite lovely."

Hale sat back and heaved a sigh. "I just wish I felt there was something to celebrate." He looked at Tree. "What do you think, old fellow? Any chance a desperate brother-in-law could change your mind?"

Freddie gave her husband a warning look. Tree cleared his throat and said, "Freddie's right, Hale. I am a fish out of water here. At least in Florida I'm on somewhat familiar ground. In London, I'm not even sure where I would even begin."

"I can tell you where," Hale said. "You would begin at Trellick Tower."

"Why would Tree start there?" Freddie asked.

"Because, as it happens, Katrina lives at the Trellick Tower, the same place I've arranged for you and Freddie to stay for the next month. You could keep an eye on her. See where she goes. What she does."

"Sorry, Hale," Tree said. "If I thought it would

help, I'd give it a try. But I doubt it will, and I'm certainly not the man for the job."

Hale issued another sigh, accompanied by a dismissive wave of his hand. "Very well, then. I suppose I understand. You can't say I didn't try."

Freddie leaned forward, placing her hand on her brother's. "Hale, it'll be all right."

Hale rallied and said, "I'm glad the two of you are here, and I apologize if I've put you in an awkward position."

Freddie squeezed Hale's hand. "I love you brother, you know that."

"I know," Hale said.

She took her hand away, smiling. "Now let's get to the really important question."

"What's that?" Hale asked.

"What's for dessert?"

Everyone forced a laugh.

4

In the taxi back to Trellick Tower, Freddie turned to Tree and asked, "What are you thinking?"

"I'm not thinking about anything."

"Yes, you are. You're thinking about Katrina Phillips."

"I am not," Tree protested.

"I can hear the machinery turning between your ears. You're intrigued."

Tree had to concede he was, but he was not about to admit that to his wife. He said, "Do you have any idea what Derek does for a living?"

Freddie shrugged. "Some sort of entrepreneurial business thing, I think, although I'm not sure. Hale doesn't talk about it."

"The enigmatic son marrying the mysterious femme fatale," Tree said.

"You think she looks like a femme fatale?"

"I think she looks like she fell off the cover of one of those pulp fiction mysteries I read as a kid."

"The pulp mysteries that corrupted your life, and drew you to the dark place where private eyes wore trench coats and women were babes in expensive lingerie."

"Those are the ones," Tree said.

The London sun made an appearance as they arrived at Trellick Tower, paid the taxi driver, and then walked toward the entrance. Next to the apartment complex, a clutch of Middle Eastern men were scattered along the street outside a café, chatting and smoking. However, the police who earlier had flooded the area were gone.

"I'd almost forgotten about that body," Freddie said. "I wonder if they know what happened."

"Murder most foul, as Agatha Christie would say."

"You read Agatha Christie?" Freddie sounded surprised.

"Not really," Tree said. "I found her and most of the other English detective novelists too tame. I preferred the American mean streets, not stately mansions occupied by the wealthy landed gentry dressing for dinner before the detective solves the murder with everyone gathered in the library."

"Maybe it isn't as nasty as murder," Freddie said.

"What do you think it would be?"

"Maybe the man they found had a heart attack. Or committed suicide."

"A case for Scotland Yard," Tree said.

"As long as a crazed killer isn't loose in our neighborhood."

"Crazed killers stick to America, they don't come here," Tree said.

They were supposed to use their key fob in order to buzz themselves into the building, but the main entrance door was open. The security guard behind the desk in the lobby waved at them. The elevator arrived along with the electronic voice of the anonymous English woman with perfect diction who once again announced, "Doors are opening." As soon as they entered, the elevator, the courteous English woman assured that "Doors are closing." And so they were.

"So tell me what did you think?" Tree broke the silence.

"The dead body found outside our apartment building?"

"You know what I mean."

"My brother has always been manipulative and slightly paranoid," Freddie said. "That's probably why he's made so much money. But honestly, this is taking manipulation and paranoia to new levels, even for him."

"There could be more to it," Tree said.

Freddie gave him a look he had seen many times before, the one that signaled she didn't like the way this conversation was going. "What do you mean?" she said.

"That he's not telling us everything," Tree said.

"Okay," Freddie said slowly. "Why do you think that, Mr. Detective?"

"Just a hunch. But usually when you meet the beautiful young woman whom your son intends to marry, your first thought isn't that there is something wrong. Even if you don't have all the information you think you need about the fiancée, it's a big stretch, deciding to hire a private detective to discredit her."

"Is that what Hale is trying to do?"

"Most people don't hire a detective to find out the best about someone. They hire a detective because they suspect the worst. Question is, what does Hale suspect?"

"I'm tempted to say you don't know my brother," Freddie replied. "But I see your point. Maybe there are things he isn't telling us."

"Like about Derek, for instance."

"What do you mean?"

"You're not sure what Derek does. Hale doesn't say much about it. Now this mysterious woman. Could be that this has more to do with Derek, and what he does or does not do, than it does with Katrina Phillips.

"Not that it makes any difference to you."

"No, of course not."

"Quit saying 'of course not.' It makes me nervous."

"No," Tree said. "It doesn't make any difference."

"Because you're not getting yourself involved in this. Right?"

"Of course not."

Freddie gave him another look. "Tree."

"I said I'm not."

"I don't trust you," Freddie said.

Tree was saved from having to answer by the courteous English woman's perfect voice announcing that the elevator had reached the twenty-seventh floor, and, further, that the doors were opening.

They went through the double fire doors and made their way along the passageway leading to their apartment. The windows on their left provided a view of row upon row of neatly laid out houses, stretching toward London's southern reaches.

Tree went to work employing the two keys to open

the door to flat number one hundred and eighty-four. Inside, Freddie threw herself onto the sofa. "I don't know why, but I always feel drained after my encounters with Hale."

"Brother-sister tension," Tree said. He went over and opened the sliding glass door to the balcony.

"You think there is tension between us?"

"You don't?"

"Maybe it's because I'm always suspicious of what Hale's motives are. This afternoon was a good example. It's lunch, but it isn't lunch. It's something else entirely. Something that serves Hale's needs of the moment."

"It's like I told you," Tree said. "He's not telling us everything."

"And just to remind you, husband dear, it's not our concern."

"I couldn't agree more."

"Another line of yours I hear too often."

Tree came over and lifted her off the sofa. Freddie's eyes narrowed. "What are you up to?"

"It's London," Tree said. "What do you think I'm up to?"

"No good, I'm guessing."

"Nothing could be further from the truth."

"Yet another line I hear far too often. Is sex legal in England?"

"Absolutely. Members of the House of Lords do it all the time."

"Let's try to keep this out of the tabloids," Freddie said.

"I'll do my best," Tree said. "But I'm afraid I can't guarantee anything."

They were in the bedroom when Freddie's telephone buzzed. "We could ignore that," Tree said.

"We could," Freddie said. "But maybe we shouldn't."

Naked, Freddie crossed to the chest of drawers to her phone, Tree admiring her remarkable curves. She looked at the readout. "It's Hale."

Freddie swiped the phone open and put it on speaker mode. "Hale, is everything all right?"

"Bedlam. Absolute bedlam."

"What's happened?"

"The wedding is off, I'm afraid."

Freddie said, "What do you mean, off?"

"Derek called a few minutes after you left. The wedding has been cancelled. That dreadful, duplicitous woman has walked away from my son."

5

Morning rain and mist hid the view of the city as Tree slipped out of bed. Freddie, stirred, opened her eyes, closed them again, and announced she was too tired to even think about getting out of bed. "Must be the jet lag," she murmured. "A really, really good husband would bring his poor, exhausted wife coffee."

"Fortunately for you, I fall into the category of good, not necessarily *really* good, but good enough to get you coffee," said Tree.

"My hero," Freddie said.

"And in the rain, too."

"A saint as well as a hero," she mumbled.

"You chose well," said Tree.

"That's what I tell skeptics."

"The army of skeptics," Tree said.

The coffee maker in the kitchen had defeated their efforts to make it work. Therefore, because he was, as advertised, at least for the moment, "a really, really good husband," he would go down to their favorite coffee spot, the Golborne Deli, and bring back two lattes.

The police had identified the body found in Meanwhile Gardens, BBC radio news reported as Tree pulled on sweat pants, a hoodie, and slipped into a pair of worn sneakers he had packed with the vague intention of going jogging while in London. He grabbed his wallet, the keys, and, almost as an afterthought, the Oyster card that would provide him access to the city's transit.

The deceased, said the BBC news reader, was Martin Bennett, age forty-four. Police sources said Bennett was known to them. The possibility of foul play had not been ruled out.

"Did you hear that?" Tree called into the bedroom. "It's foul play, no doubt about it."

"That's not what the radio is saying," Freddie said, emerging, hair tousled, still in her flannel pajamas.

"Known to police. Body found in a park just around the corner from here. This isn't Agatha Christie. This is *Lock, Stock, and Two Smoking Barrels*. This is Bob Hoskins in *The Long Good Friday*, Michael Caine in *Get Carter.*"

"You've lost me," Freddie said.

"Great British gangster films. Evidence that the Brits can walk the mean streets when they have to."

"This is real life, Tree," Freddie said. "It's not a British gangster movie."

"Real life is the place where people get themselves killed."

"I'm hoping it's not-so-foul play," said Freddie.

Tree made a harrumphing sound before saying that he would be back with coffee in a few minutes.

"Don't get lost," Freddie said.

"It's just down the street. How could I get lost?"

Freddie rolled her eyes.

On the elevator, Tree thought again about the cancelled wedding. Freddie had spoken to Hale a couple of times the night before with updates on the calamity that had befallen the family.

According to Hale, there was no satisfactory explanation for what had happened. Katrina Phillips apparently decided it was better to end things now rather than make a terrible mistake.

Derek was devastated, according to Hale. As for himself, he wasn't sure whether to be pleased or furious that his son had been betrayed. Perhaps a bit of both. Certainly Katrina had confirmed his worst fears.

Outside, the rain came steadily down. They said it was summer in London. They lied, Tree concluded, as he dashed west along Golborne Road. He crossed the bridge over the train tracks and then continued along the street, mostly deserted at this hour. However, at the Golborne Deli, their breakfast destination of choice while in London, the rough, inviting interior was filled with patrons stopping for coffee and a croissant.

Tree stood in a line backed up to the door. The tables were also filled, mostly with couples sipping large bowls of coffee while they inspected morning papers. The coke-snorting Lord and his ladies were splashed across tabloids. Martin Bennett who had died just up the street from here, had failed, from what Tree could see, to make headlines.

Pretty young servers in black swerved through the crowd balancing trays filled with croissants and toast, scrambled eggs on wooden plates, steaming porridge decorated with strawberries and bananas. Good-natured chatter rose in the warming interior while the rain pounded outside. One of the servers swept past

asking what he would like. Two medium lattes to go. She rewarded him with a fleeting smile.

A woman with a Styrofoam coffee cup brushed against him. He said, "Excuse me."

A beautiful young woman. A beautiful young woman who looked startlingly familiar.

Katrina Phillips at the Golborne Deli, hurrying out the door.

6

Katrina beneath a rain-streaked black umbrella, striding along Golborne toward Portobello Road. Katrina in a beige-colored raincoat, perfect, Tree thought, for a mystery woman disappearing into London mist.

Not all that surprising to encounter her, he supposed. After all, according to Hale Stayner, she resided in the same Trellick Tower as he and Freddie. That's what Hale had hoped for, he supposed. Now it had happened. Here she was a half a block or so ahead of him. Tree didn't think about it. He followed her.

By the time Katrina reached Portobello Road the rain was reduced to a summer drizzle. She turned south, taking down the umbrella, all but disappearing into the swelling crowds swarming the street inspecting the stalls set up for the Saturday market, buyers and sellers alike braving the rain.

Tree struggled through the throngs, the road curving beneath a railroad overpass. For a time, he lost her, but then just when he thought she had disappeared amid the streams of people, he caught sight of her again. She did not stop to inspect the stalls jammed along the street, the collections of classic rock 'n' roll CDs, the inexpensive shrink-wrapped shirts, the cut-rate telephone protectors or even the enticing pan of steaming paella. Katrina was oblivious to all of it, glancing neither left nor right, ploughing ahead, a young woman on a mission.

But what mission? That's what he hoped to find out, wasn't it? Unless, of course, there was no mission, simply Katrina walking in London on a rainy morning. Freddie would say he was being ridiculous, and Freddie was probably right. Nonetheless, he kept Katrina in view as she came to the bottom of Portobello Road where shops with brightly colored storefronts displayed the expensive goods critics said were ruining the neighborhood.

Katrina veered onto Pembridge Road and followed it to Notting Hill Gate. There she stopped, standing expectantly, looking at her watch from time to time, peering along the tree-shaded street, as if anxious for the bus to arrive.

Tree watched from outside a nearby bookshop, pretending to poke through bins containing discounted books. The red double decker arrived and she got on. Tree hurried over, climbed aboard, and smacked his Oyster Card against the yellow card reader. The doors hushed shut. Another of the many disembodied voices that lived in London elevators and on the city's various forms of transit, announced the next stop, and the bus started forward. Tree grabbed at a yellow strap, bracing himself against the sway of the bus, a few feet from the seated Katrina Phillips.

As the bus moved along, Tree glanced in her direction. Yes, she was certainly beautiful. Otherwise, it was hard to tell much about her.

After only two stops, she rose abruptly and exited the bus. Tree waited a moment and then followed.

The sky above Kensington Gardens was the color of slate, the rain threatening to return any time. Katrina marched along the wide thoroughfare cutting through the gardens until she reached a stately brick building the signs said was Kensington Palace. She went down a flight of steps into a courtyard set out with tables and chairs.

Most of the tables were occupied with that most reliable of customers, the tea-drinking tourist. Katrina managed to find an unoccupied table and sat down. She looked at her watch and frowned.

Not wanting to stick out by lingering on the periphery of what he assumed was the palace's public tea garden, Tree went through a side door into a combination cafeteria and gift shop. From here, he could keep an eye on Katrina outside in the garden while appearing to inspect Kensington Palace key chains and mugs—What? No Kensington Palace T-shirts?—and browse through a colorfully illustrated history: home to the royal family since the seventeenth century, the guide reported. Wasn't that interesting? George III, the king who lost those American colonies, housed his sixth son at the palace and the young man filled ten rooms with his collection of fifty thousand books. He also liked clocks and singing birds. The singing birds flew around the fifty thousand books.

Tree looked up from his reading as a tall man in a blue pinstriped suit balanced two tea cups as he moved away from the cashier and headed toward the exit. In

his late sixties, Tree guessed, white hair pushed back from an impressively haggard visage, the sort of face, Tree imagined, at gleaming conference tables negotiating peace treaties on behalf of the British Empire. Or watching birds fly around fifty thousand-book libraries.

Tree watched him cross the garden to place the tea cups in front of Katrina. She smiled her thanks as the man in the pinstriped suit heaved himself into the empty chair beside her. He gave Katrina a dour smile.

Tree's cellphone vibrated in his pocket, causing him to jump. He swiped the phone open.

"What happened to you?" Freddie said.

"I'm okay," Tree said.

"The fact that you're okay is beside the point." Freddie sounded cross. "I'm sitting here alone in this apartment dying for a coffee. Where are you?"

"I'm at Kensington Palace."

"This isn't funny, Tree."

"I'm serious. I'm at Kensington Palace. Don't Kate and William live here?"

"They moved out," Freddie said. "Kate didn't like being stared at all the time."

"That explains why I haven't seen them."

"Tree, what are you doing?"

"If I tell you what I'm doing, you're liable to kill me."

"I won't kill you," Freddie said. "Probably just maim you a bit."

Tree lowered his voice and said, "I'm following Katrina Phillips."

"What?" The note of astonishment in Freddie's voice was unmistakable.

"Derek's fiancée."

"I know who she is, Tree. The question is, why?" The astonishment had been replaced by exasperation.

Through the doorway to the garden, Tree could see the pinstriped man remove a thick business envelope from inside his suit jacket. He placed it on the table beside Katrina's tea cup.

"Listen," Tree said to Freddie. "I'm going to have to call you back."

"What's happened, Tree? What are you doing?" A demanding edge to her voice.

"I'll get back to you."

He closed the phone. Out in the garden, Katrina kept her eyes on the envelope. The pinstriped man watched her carefully.

Tree hit the camera app on his phone and stepped outside, raising the phone and taking a picture just as Katrina picked up the envelope.

Katrina looked straight at him as his camera clicked again. The pinstriped man said, "That bloody arse just took our photograph!"

7

The pinstriped man leapt from his chair, charging over to Tree. "What the bloody hell do you think you're doing?" he demanded. His dour face had reddened so that he looked less the diplomat negotiating peace, more like a hard old general about to go to war.

"I'm taking a picture of the garden," Tree managed to sputter.

"Like bloody hell you are," snapped the pinstriped man. "You were shooting us. Who sent you? What's this about?"

"It's all right, Gerrold." Katrina was at the pinstriped man's elbow. "I know who he is. It's fine."

The warlike general's face took on a sheen of confusion. "What's that supposed to mean? You know this fellow?"

"I know what he's doing here. Let me take care of it."

"This is not part of our agreement," Gerrold said.

"I understand, but it's not going to change anything. Discretion is guaranteed, I told you that."

"I know what you told me," Gerrold said. "But I must now try to reassure very angry and powerful people in this very building that this is over—that your assurances can be counted on."

"Tell your people not to worry," Katrina said in a calm voice. "Our business is finished and there is nothing more for you to be concerned about. Let me deal with my friend and his camera."

Gerrold's eyes gleamed out from beneath heavy lids. His jowls shook a bit, but the panicky look was gone. "I must trust you Katrina," he said. "I don't like it, but I have to trust you."

"I appreciate that, Gerrold."

"I hope my faith is not misplaced."

Gerrold gave Tree one more withering look before turning on his heel and walking away into the palace, leaving Tree with Katrina. She focused cool gray eyes on him.

"You're not very discreet are you?" A perfectly modulated British-accent inflected voice.

"I was taking a picture of the garden, that's all," Tree repeated.

"Let's sit over here and have a talk, yeah?"

Frantically fumbling in his mind for something that might sound like a reasonable explanation for his presence, he followed Katrina back to the same table she had recently occupied with her friend Gerrold. "Sit down," she said.

He did as she demanded. She sat across from him, wrapping slim fingers around her tea cup. "I still haven't finished my tea," she said.

"Yes," was all he could think to say.

"Do you want something? she asked. "The tea here's very good."

"No, I'm fine," Tree said.

"I know you've been following me." She said it in a

casual way that suggested she was followed all the time and accepted it as the natural state of things.

"You're not very good at it," she added after taking a sip of tea.

"I guess not," was all Tree could come up with.

"Who sent you? Leo Skeleton?"

Tree didn't know what to say.

"I thought so," she said with satisfaction. "It's not necessary. I told him that. He can trust me. He doesn't need to have me followed."

"No," Tree said.

"But here you are. Following me, yeah?"

"Here I am." Tree gave what he was certain was the weakest of grins.

"I'm surprised he didn't send Ronnie and Todd."

"He didn't," Tree said.

"I guess it's because I would know them." She grinned. "And now I know you, don't I?"

"Yes, you do," Tree agreed.

"Leo really is a right bastard, yeah?"

"If you say so," Tree said.

"I know you work for him but come on, you've got to admit he's a bit of a creep."

"He pays me, that's what counts." Tree trying to sound tough, like the kind of guy who would get paid to follow beautiful women.

Those gray eyes studied him intently. Unblinking. "Okay. Tell you what. You come along with me, yeah? That way you can keep an eye on me, and I don't have to be fretting about you trailing after me."

Tree didn't have to pretend to look surprised.

She grinned and the light danced in her eyes. "There, I've shaken you up a bit, yeah? You weren't expecting that."

"No, I wasn't," Tree said truthfully.

"Good. Now since we're going to be together for the next while, you'd better tell me your name."

Tree thought about this a moment. What kind of name would he have? Tough guy name: "John Rio," he said.

"Well, John Rio, what are you? American?"

"By the dawn's early light."

"American John Rio. Let's be off, yeah?"

"Where are we going?"

Another grin. "That's what you're about to find out."

8

They came out onto Kensington Road. The sky had cleared sufficiently to give the sun a fighting chance. Katrina hailed a taxi. Once inside, she gave the driver an address on Piccadilly.

"Sure you wouldn't like to tell me where we're going?" Tree said.

"And spoil the mystery? I don't think so," Katrina said. "It's too much fun this way."

The taxi passed the Royal Albert Hall then onto Knightsbridge, past Hyde Park corner with the Wellington arch to the right, the traffic becoming thicker as the driver came onto Piccadilly. He made a quick U-turn, bringing the taxi to a stop outside number one hundred and ninety-five, an impressive Victorian building with BAFTA spelled out above an unprepossessing entrance door. Tree found himself entering the headquarters of the British Academy of Film and Television Arts.

He followed Katrina up a flight of marble stairs past a landing adorned with a reproduction of BAFTA's iconic golden mask (was that a look of knowing disdain as Tree passed?) to a reception desk. Katrina told the attendant they had an appointment with someone named Mabel Cadogan. She was signed in and directed to the bar area where a very tall, slim woman draped in tones of black and gray waved at them from one of the two banquettes just inside the entrance. Mabel Cadogan's thin line of a mouth grimaced when she saw Tree.

"I thought you were coming alone, dear," she said in plumy tones as Katrina reached the booth.

"John Rio, this is Mabel Cadogan," Katrina said. "John is an American."

"That doesn't explain what he's doing here."

"Ensuring everything runs smoothly."

Mabel said, "Very well. Don't just stand there, dear. Sit down. Sit down."

Katrina and Tree squeezed into the booth. Tree glanced around. Posters from director David Lean's films were mounted high on the surrounding walls. The lovers in *Ryan's Daughter* were oblivious to the world; Alec Guinness peered down with a jaundiced eye from the *Bridge on the River Kwai*.

Mabel leaned forward, eyes fixed on Katrina. "Let me tell you something. Have you got a moment?"

"Certainly," Katrina said politely.

"This happened many, many years ago, of course. I was a young actress just arrived in London from Oxford. A bit of a trollop, if you want to know the truth. Up for just about any adventure in this wild and wicked city. I ended up at someone's weekend party in Hampstead. Larry Olivier was there and naturally there was great excitement. I was quite intrigued, I must say. He was older then, but still very handsome. I liked older men." She smiled. "I liked men, when it came right down to it.

"Somehow Larry—such a devil—got me into

a pantry. I wasn't objecting a great deal. All sorts of groping and heavy breathing ensued. He wanted me to come back to his place in Eaton Square so off we went. His wife, Viv, was waiting when we arrived. She didn't seem at all perturbed that her husband had brought home a young actress, eager to experience just about anything.

"Well, Larry opened the champagne. One thing led to another and we all ended up in a bed the size of a football field. It was, I must say, quite a night. There I was naked between Hamlet and Scarlett O'Hara. Not everyone can say that."

"Certainly not," Katrina said.

"The point of all this is, it was the three of us. A scandal, I suppose, except it wasn't. Everyone parted the next morning with smiles. No guilt, no recriminations, and nothing in the papers. Nobody's career was in jeopardy. So there's the difference, right? Back then it was three people in bed. Today it's a career-destroying scandal."

"What can I tell you, Mabel?" Katrina said after a moment of uneasy silence. "That was then. This is now. The times are much different."

"Yes, they are, aren't they?" She gave a deep sigh. "Do you want anything? I can go to the bar and order you something."

"I think we're fine, Mabel. I'm under time constraints today so it's probably best to conclude our business as quickly as possible."

Mabel's thin mouth tightened more. "You want payment."

"Then you'll be finished with this and we can all get about our lives," Katrina said.

Mabel narrowed flinty eyes at Katrina and said, "As I said earlier, I was a bit of a tramp in my youth. I make no apologies. However, my daughter is not a tramp."

"No one is suggesting she is," Katrina said.

Mabel leaned forward, lowered her voice, eyes steady on Katrina. "Melanie, has worked very hard to make a successful career for herself, and now you come along and threaten to destroy everything she's worked for."

"I am not destroying anything," Katrina replied. "I am merely the messenger. What Melanie does or does not do with the information that's been provided is up to her."

"That's ridiculous and you know it." Mabel's voice rose in anger. "What's she supposed to do? What choice does she have? She must pay you bastards."

"We've been through this, Mabel," Katrina said patiently. "I'm here today because you said you had made your decision. Have you now decided something different?"

"No, of course not." Mabel glared some more and then lifted a paisley tote bag onto the seat beside her. She opened it up, fished around, and then brought out a white business envelope. She dropped it on the table in front of Katrina. "There you go, dear. There's your blood money."

Katrina lifted up her shoulder bag, unzipped it, and dropped the envelope inside.

"Aren't you going to count it?" Mabel sneered.

"I trust you, Mabel."

"The question is, can I trust you?"

"You can trust the people with whom you have been dealing. You have made the necessary payment; they will stick by their agreement."

"This is all so reprehensible," Mabel said.

"But now it is over," Katrina said, sliding out from the booth, "and it's time for us to leave." She got to her feet. Tree joined her.

"Goodbye, Mabel," Katrina said. "Please wish your daughter all the best in her future endeavors. I'm a great fan of her work."

She turned and started away. Mabel called in a curiously gentle voice, "Katrina, dear…"

Katrina turned to find Mabel on her feet, her long face haggard and set. She took a couple of steps forward, raised a bony hand and slapped Katrina hard across the face, causing gasps from nearby tables.

"Bitch," Mabel said.

9

Back on the street, Katrina paused and took a deep breath, the side of her face reddening where Mabel Cadogan had struck her.

"Are you all right?" Tree asked.

She gulped in some air. Her eyes were unnaturally bright. "Of course I'm all right, why wouldn't I be?"

"You seem a little shaken up."

"Not feeling sorry for me, are you John Rio?"

"Never crossed my mind," Tree said.

"Just make sure you tell Leo, if he asks, that I took the blows, got the job done, yeah?"

"Sure, I'll tell him. You're doing a great job."

"All right, let's get going,"

"Where to?"

"Tube station," she called, scurrying along the street.

———

Tree followed her out of the South Kensington Underground, hurrying to keep up as she moved briskly along Cromwell Road, dodging herds of tourists. The tourists looked slightly dazed and a trifle lost. Karina moved adroitly through them, the streetwise Londoner who knew just how to handle invaders.

"Are you in a hurry?" he called to her.

She answered without bothering to turn her head. "Not particularly."

"Then if you're not in a hurry, you might consider slowing down."

"Out of shape then are you?"

"I didn't think so until I met you."

She gave him a triumphant grin but dropped her pace so that they walked together. "Don't you think you're a little old for this sort of thing?"

"What sort of thing is that?"

"Following people around."

"It's an ageless profession," Tree said.

"I wonder about that," Katrina said. "Are you a gangster, yeah? Did they send an American gangster to make sure I behaved?"

"Are you misbehaving?"

"What do you think?"

"I'm not sure what to think," he said, truthfully.

Katrina turned a corner and there, dominating the block, the great stone pile of the Victoria and Albert Museum. "Come along," she called to him. "Here's your chance to experience some British culture. Make a better man out of you."

Tree wondered if that was possible.

A vast, domed rotunda with its great arches and proud Grecian columns bespoke the grandeur of an empire long gone but living still in the elegant bones of the Victoria and Albert.

"The museum contains nearly five million objects," Katrina said, as if to confirm the importance promised by the rotunda.

"You don't say," said Tree.

"It's been here since 1851," Katrina continued, "but they didn't actually rename it the Victoria and Albert Museum until 1899. The name change marked Queen Victoria's last public appearance."

He made an isn't-that-interesting sound as Katrina scurried through the gift shop, Tree heaving along behind, and then outside into a sunlit courtyard. A man rose from a nearby table when he saw her. Like Gerrold from Kensington Palace, he too was a smartly dressed patrician, although younger and much slimmer, brown hair, graying at the temples. He gave Katrina a wane smile. "There you are," he said. "I had just about given up hope."

"Never give up hope, Gavin," Katrina said.

"No, I suppose not," the tall man named Gavin said enigmatically. His hooded eyes focused on Tree. "I thought you were coming alone."

"I never agreed to anything like that," Katrina said.

"Then please identify this rather rough-looking chap."

"My security," Katrina answered. "In case you decide to throw a punch at me, yeah?"

"Alas, I am far too much of a gentleman," Gavin said.

"You sound disappointed," she said with a coquettish smile.

"Yes, I suppose I am," he said seriously.

He reached inside his suit jacket and withdrew what was by now a familiar thick white envelope. He handed it to Katrina. "There you go. I presume this concludes our business?"

"It's all here?"

"Would you expect anything else?"

"So this journey has come to a successful conclusion for both of us."

"Not quite, Katrina." Gavin's face had become solemn, his manner expectant.

"Yes, I must give you something."

"Yes, you must," Gavin said dryly.

She rummaged in her shoulder bag and withdrew a manila envelope and gave it to Gavin. He looked at it and Tree thought he would open the envelope. Instead, he rapped his knuckles against it and said to Katrina, "There are no copies?"

"You have my word."

"I'm not sure that your word is worth anything at this point," Gavin said.

"I'm sorry you feel that way," Katrina said, not sounding at all sorry.

"You've seen the papers the last few days? What they've done to Lord Butler?"

"I've seen what Lord Butler has done to himself."

"You may not be aware of it, but just before coming here I received word that Butler's wife found his body this morning. It's early, but it looks as though he committed suicide."

"I'm sorry, Gavin, really I am," Katrina said. "But we both know it didn't have to come this. None of it needed to happen, if only Lord Butler had listened to reason."

"You should know, those photographs you have—"

Katrina cut him off: "I don't have anything, Gavin."

"Those photographs were faked."

"I have no idea what you're talking about," Katrina said.

"Then a word of advice if I may."

"Oh, dear," said Katrina. "Advice. I never like that word."

"You shouldn't be mixed up in this nonsense." He nodded at Tree. "You shouldn't be mixed up with characters like him. I would have thought better of you."

"I appreciate that, Gavin. But let me say that we are both pawns in someone else's game. There are unsavory characters on both sides." She nodded at Tree. "Worse even than John Rio here."

"You would know more about that," Gavin said with a tight smile.

"This is a business arrangement, pure and simple. You have what you want. We have what we want."

"My prayer is that after this you will be able to sleep nights."

"Then I will pray for you as well, Gavin. And while I'm praying you might advise your employer not to get mixed up in this sort of thing again."

Gavin opened his mouth to answer, decided against it, and shrugged. "These are secrets that should never leave a man's bedroom," he said.

"Or a woman's for that matter. But they did, and here we are."

"Goodbye, Katrina." Gavin turned, and without another word went back across the courtyard.

Two little boys, not disposed to culture, raced past. Katrina ignored them. She stood very still, not saying anything. Tree saw her swallow a couple of times, and then appear to shake off Gavin's admonishing words. She turned to Tree. "You see, I shouldn't be mixed up with characters like you."

"Apparently not," Tree said.

"But it's too late to be crying over that particular glass of spilled milk. Come along. Time to leave."

They went outside, down the steps onto the wide pavement. She came to a stop at the curb and turned to him. The light shifted across the perfection of those cheekbones and that smooth, pale skin. Was Tree's heart beating a little faster as he met her gaze? No, it couldn't be.

"So there you have it, John Rio," she said. "Everything on the up and up. You can report back to Leo and tell him he doesn't have to worry about me." She held out her hand. "This is where we say goodbye."

Curiously, instead of being relieved that he could now safely make his escape, Tree did not want to leave. "Are you sure you're going to be all right?"

Not exactly a John Rio question and she responded with a curious look. "Why shouldn't I be?"

"You know, it's like that character back there said, you being involved in this. Are you sure you know what you're doing?"

"That's what you're here to find out, isn't it?"

"Yeah," he said, trying to sound gruff. "I guess it is."

"Tell Leo that I know exactly what I'm doing, if that's what he's worried about."

"It's not Leo who's worried," Tree said.

"Yeah?" Then who?"

"Maybe it's me," Tree said.

"You?" She looked at him for a time before she smiled and said, "Well, I appreciate your concern. But here's what we do now. You go your way and I'll go mine. Then neither one of us has to worry if we're 'all right,' as you put it."

"I guess you're pretty tough."

The smile was replaced by an unexpected flutter of uncertainty before her face hardened and she said, "Tough has nothing to do with it. It's the job. I get it done—as you can see. That's the end of it."

Tree was concentrating on Katrina and therefore didn't notice the blue van swerve to the curb. But she saw it, and her face went blank. Tree focused in time to see the van's side door slam open and three men jump out. All three wore Balaclavas. Tree had a fleeting thought that it was a cool summer in London, but not *that* cool.

What happened next occurred in a series of flashes, bursts of activity unfolding so quickly they blurred the landscape of Tree's vision: one of the men grabbing Katrina, a Balaclava-clad figure lunging for him, a black object raised in a thick fist.

And then familiar lancing pain and bursting

stars followed by the end of everything—the black-out with which Tree was all too familiar.

10

Now, the return from the dead.

The slowly dawning realization that you have not been killed by the hard blow you received. There was pain, certainly, but looking at it optimistically, as Tree tended to do, that was good news; it meant you were regaining consciousness, and from that you could surmise you were still alive. In pain, but alive.

He sat up slowly, head hurting—naturally. One of the requirements of the job was that the employee—Tree Callister—take many blows to the head. He had already begun the complicated business of processing a sense of where he was—a cabin of some sort from the look of things, a cabin tipped to the expressionist angles of *The Cabinet of Dr. Caligari.*

He managed to elevate himself to an upright position, and that led to another series of complications, these dealing with the business of placing one's feet on the floor, at the same time holding one's head in a vain attempt to control the pain and clear the stars. He heard himself breathing hard, panicky breathing, he thought, the gasping for air that comes when you are in pain, have no idea where you are, and, oh yes, are scared out of your mind.

Sitting up, he could see a low ceiling, shelves filled with books, a desk overflowing with papers and files, old comfortable furniture that didn't fit the space.

He heard footsteps. A man rose up a staircase. Reaching the top of the stairs, he saw that Tree was awake. After fumbling in his pocket the man pulled out a gun. Tree groaned inwardly. How did he constantly get himself into circumstances where he ended up with a sore head facing someone pointing a gun?

The man with the gun was young, dressed in a torso-fitting black T-shirt and matching black slacks. He had sleepy Robert Mitchum eyes behind eyeglasses with bamboo frames. His dark blond hair was neatly combed to either side of a part. Perfectly aligned features lent him the bland, vaguely androgynous look of a male model. In the movies he would be the fresh-faced young fellow just starting out in the world. Real life and a gun made him look a lot more dangerous—and familiar.

Tree had never met Hale Stayner's son. But he had seen the photos, and so he recognized Derek as he said in a slurry voice, "The tide's out, old fellow." He stumbled a bit crossing the room.

Tree looked at him. "Careful with that gun," he said.

"That's why the barge is listing," Derek added.

"Barge?" Tree said. "This is a barge? On the Thames?"

"Of course, it's on the Thames. Where else would it be?"

"So when the tide goes out, what? You hit people over the head and pull a gun on them?"

Derek's bland handsomeness betrayed no emotion. "I haven't been well lately. Not sleeping properly. I took some medication earlier."

"You probably shouldn't be operating heavy machinery or using a gun," Tree said.

Derek looked down at the gun in his hand. "It's a German Mauser. Very rare. They don't make them any more. I like to point it at people."

"Do you?"

"People I don't like."

"I'm a very likable fellow," Tree said.

"If you're so likable why are you sleeping with my fiancée?"

That caused Tree to jerk his head, a demonstration of amazement that sent electric bolts shooting into his brain. Through a white drizzle of hurt, he heard himself say, "What?"

"Also, why don't you tell me, while you're at it, how Katrina and Leo are cheating me." "These are questions you had better ask Katrina."

"Katrina's not here, you are, old fellow. So let's have some answers. "

Katrina wasn't there? What had happened to Katrina?

Out loud, Tree said, "I'm not sure what kind of answers you're looking for."

"Start with how long you've been sleeping with her. Well, I suppose you're not actually sleeping, are you?"

Sleeping with Katrina? Tree thought of blurting out the truth. Except the truth sounded like a bad lie. Besides, depending on what Derek was involved in— and a guy standing unsteadily, holding a gun, is likely not involved in anything good—it might be wise to keep quiet. Telling the truth, he had discovered, tended to get you killed. Lying through your teeth could save your skin.

For now, he remained John Rio, tough guy, possibly duplicitous, accused of being Katrina's lover. As unlikely as that seemed.

Tree said, "What makes you think I'm sleeping with Katrina?"

A tight grimace marred the perfection of Derek's features. "A week ago she was going to marry me. Everything was set. Then out of nowhere she cancels, and the next thing she turns up with you. Starts to fall into place, don't you think?"

"I didn't turn up with her. I was standing on the sidewalk when a van pulled up and guys wearing Balaclavas jumped out and hit me on the head. I presume you're responsible for that."

Derek chose not to respond. Instead, he said, "Explain what you were doing together."

"Believe me, it had nothing to do with love," Tree said.

"No? What's it got to do with?"

"With Leo being suspicious," Tree said.

"Leo?" Derek abruptly looked less sleepy and a lot more interested. "You mean Leo Skeleton?"

Tree nodded. "Leo wanting to make sure everything is all right."

"Leo is a son of a bitch," Derek said.

"Tell me something I don't know," Tree said.

Derek looked even tenser. "Leo ruined my life."

"Leo likes to do that." When you are in a tight spot, and lying, Tree had long ago decided, the best thing is to always agree with the person you are lying to.

"What does Leo think? That Katrina is cheating him?"

"How do I know?" Tree said, feeling more comfortable now that he was back in John Rio's shoes. "Leo doesn't explain things. He just tells me what to do."

"Okay, what did Leo tell you to do?"

"He told me to follow the woman. Like I said, nothing to do with love."

"But you weren't following her." Derek, accusatory again. "You were *with* her, old fellow."

Tree made a show of shrugging. "What can I tell you? She made me; my cover was blown. Next thing she's in my face saying I might as well just come along with her, and that way I could see what she was doing and report back to Leo."

That seemed to make Derek relax a bit. To Tree's relief, he lowered the gun. "So that bastard Leo's behind this."

"I don't know what Leo's behind or isn't behind," Tree said—the truest sentence he had uttered all afternoon. "All I know is what he told me to do. That's when I ended up here with a bump on my head and a jealous guy with a gun acting stupid."

"Hey, watch it," Derek said in a threatening tone.

"Come on, get real," Tree said, now full John Rio. "What are you going to do? Shoot me for calling you stupid?"

"Don't tempt me," Derek said. "I'm not well. I can't be responsible for my actions."

But he didn't shoot Tree. He stumbled a bit and then slumped into a canvas-back chair. The Mauser pistol in his hand, but the air had gone out of him. His voice was a slurry mumble. "I hate Leo. Leo really messed up things for me."

"How did he do that?" Tree asked.

"Katrina. My father warned me about her. Of course I didn't listen. Never listen to the old man." He focused glazed eyes on Tree. "That's not her real name, you know."

"No, I didn't know," Tree said.

"Miriam, if you can believe it. A little girl from Northern England, determined to make good in London. Well, I suppose she's done all right for herself. Women like that always do, don't they?"

"I don't know," Tree said. "Do they?"

Derek didn't reply for a time. Then he shrugged. "What do I know about women? Nothing, it turns out. A better offer, I suppose. Isn't that how you lose things? Someone comes along with a better offer?"

"What kind of better offer?" Tree asked.

Derek's eyes narrowed. "Too many questions, old fellow." Abruptly the gun was pointing at Tree again. "You're not a liar, are you?"

"Not me," Tree said.

"Can't stand liars. Katrina's a liar. All lies. Told me nothing but lies."

"You've got the gun, friend. Why should I lie to you?"

Derek dismissively waved the hand holding the Mauser. "I don't know. I don't know anything anymore."

"Where's Katrina?" Tree asked.

Derek gazed at him with dull, disinterested eyes. "That liar? She is a liar."

"Do you have her here?"

"I don't *have* her. No one *has* Katrina, old fellow. Not even Leo. He may think he has her, but take it from me, he doesn't."

"Your guys shoved her into a van just before they slugged me. What happened to her?"

"What can I tell you? Katrina does what Katrina does. Gone. In a puff of smoke."

"So what are you going to do now?"

Derek looked at Tree and a sly smile made its way across his face. "Maybe I'll shoot you."

"You keep saying that," Tree said.

"I'm mulling over the possibility."

"I don't think that's a very good idea." Tree tried to make the words come out calmly.

"I'm not so sure about that." Derek once again discovered the presence of the gun in his hand. He appeared surprised to be holding it. "What the hell," he said.

"I can't say for sure," Tree said, his eyes on the gun, "but I have a suspicion Leo wouldn't like you shooting his employees."

"I hate Leo. Who gives a damn about Leo?"

Derek fell back in the chair. "I'm not feeling so well. Dizzy in fact. Need a little medicinal relief. I'm under a doctor's care, what with one thing and another."

"I'm sorry to hear that," Tree said.

"Just going to close my eyes. Then we can discuss the possibility of my shooting you."

"Are you all right?'

"Fine. Tired, that's all. Maybe too much medication…"

His voice trailed off. His head fell forward onto his chest. The Mauser dropped to the floor with a clatter. He began to snore softly.

11

Tree struggled to his feet, eyes on an open doorway at the end of the cabin. He couldn't believe it. Derek sound asleep, his gun on the floor. Tree bent down to scoop up the gun. Derek issued another snore as Tree lurched out the door.

Daylight fading against darkening clouds framed the distant building blocks of the London skyline; a gangplank angled onto a quay shadowed by concrete shells camouflaged with green mesh hiding the grim skeletons of new condos rising over the Thames.

Tree sped off the gangplank, gun in hand, pumping through the darkness along the quay past those shrouded concrete monsters waiting to house the rich.

Behind him he heard an exclamation, then the sound of pounding feet coming after him—or what he imagined were pounding feet. He glanced around and, sure enough, two figures closing fast, young men, full of vast energy reserves for this sort of thing.

He, on the other hand, was old and battered. People had recently hit him on the head and thrown him into a van. Body parts he would not have imagined capable of hurting, hurt, along with all the other parts that could be expected to react badly to his various stupidities. He was here for a wedding. That's all he was supposed to do. Sit quietly watching his nephew marry. How had he managed to find himself being chased along the Thames somewhere in London? What in the name of anything that made sense was that all about?

He stumbled to a stop, breathing hard. He had the gun in his hand. He should use it, he told himself, but then there would be the endless complications that ensue when you shoot someone in a foreign country where they don't usually shoot people. You were not supposed to come to the United Kingdom and start blasting away, no matter what the reason. That was almost certainly frowned upon.

Still, his pursuers soon would be on him and they would have no second thoughts about doing serious damage to the American they were chasing.

His lungs were on fire and his head, robbed of its brief adrenalin rush, recommenced firing bolts of pain through his brain. Tree straightened and raised his gun hand, pointing in the direction of his oncoming pursuers.

The two men came to a stop as soon as they saw the gun. They were youths with shaved heads, T-shirts, intricate tattoos stitched up and down their arms, much like their tough guy American counterparts.

One of the young men said, "Here you go, mate. What you got there?"

"It's called a gun," Tree said.

"You get that from Derek, did you?"

"I want you to back off," Tree said.

"That's Derek's old Mauser pistol, I suppose," the shorter of the two young man said in a reasonable voice, "The thing about that gun, it's a collector's item, but Derek hasn't been able to find any bullets for it."

"Not that we give him bullets when he does the pills and the coke," added his pal.

"Don't make me pull the trigger to find out," Tree said.

The short young man produced a crooked smile. "Go ahead, mate. Fire away."

Tree squeezed the trigger. There was a dull click.

"Tried to tell you," said the short young man. The two started toward Tree.

Tree dropped the gun to the ground and said, "I think you've got the wrong idea about me."

"Got no idea at all, mate," said the short young man.

"I'm just a tourist visiting London," Tree said.

"Sure you are, mate, and I'm the bloody Prince of Wales." The two young men closed in on him.

Abruptly, Tree and the young men were bathed in headlights from an oncoming vehicle. Tree saw the grillwork of a Land Rover that for a wild instant he thought might run him down. But it slammed to a stop a couple of feet away. A door opened and out jumped a shadowed figure all but lost in the headlights' glow.

Tree froze in the headlights.

12

The figure floated into the wash of light and Tree saw that Katrina Phillips wore a short skirt and pointed a gun—an image right out of any number of his adolescent fantasies starring a tough, beautiful, not to mention armed, femme fatale.

"If it isn't Todd and Ronnie," Katrina said. "What happened to your Balaclavas, fellows?" Katrina said.

"Hey there, Katrina," the short young man said. "Good to see you again."

"No it isn't, Ronnie. It's never good when you see me."

"You got a point there," Ronnie agreed.

"And there are bullets in this gun," Katrina said.

"Okay," Ronnie said. "Point taken."

"When you go back to the barge, tell Derek to stop being so stupid."

"You know Derek," said the short young man called Ronnie. "When he's like this, acting stupid is sort of built into his DNA."

"Give it a try," Katrina said. "Meanwhile, leave my friend here alone."

"He's your friend is he?"

"My best pal," Katrina said. "Now get lost."

"Whether we like it or not Derek's still the boss, and he's not going to like this," said Ronnie.

"I'm past worrying about what Derek does or

doesn't like," Katrina said. She stiffened her gun hand. "Come on, fellows, off you go."

Todd and Ronnie traded glances and then started to back away. "We'll see you again soon," Ronnie said.

"Don't count on it." Katrina turned her gun toward Tree. "Get in the car," she said.

"Why does everyone point a gun at me?"

"Some of us might even shoot you. Get in the car."

He went around to the right side of the Land Rover. She shook her head in exasperation. "Wrong side, dummy."

Yes, of course. They drove on the left in this foreign, unexpectedly hostile place. He got in the other side and closed the door. Katrina was already behind the wheel shoving the gearshift into reverse. She spun the vehicle around, slammed it forward, and shot along a gravel roadway onto the street.

"How did you get away?" he asked.

She tossed him a disdainful glance. "You're kidding, yeah? Ronnie and Todd, the two wankers who work for Derek? Trying to hide under those Balaclavas? What a joke. They should have known better, but they thought you were trouble and banged you across the head. Me, at the first stoplight, I just jumped out and took off, yeah? Those poor sods had no idea what to do."

"I'm surprised you came back for me."

"Not half as surprised as I am," Katrina said. "But there you were in Derek's hands and who knows what sort of idiocy he's capable of these days. Besides, any doubts Leo has about me would go away if I rescued one of the creeps who works for him."

"You think I'm a creep?" Even if he was John Rio, tough guy, there was still something hurtful about being labelled a creep.

"You follow women around for a living. What would you call yourself?"

"A private operative doing the job he was hired to do."

"In other words, a creep." She flashed a smile. It didn't help.

"How did you know I was on that barge?"

"It's where Derek lives."

"He says you were going to marry him."

"Yeah? Well, listen, what Derek thinks in his far-too-often drug and booze-addled state, and what is actually going to happen, are two different things."

"So you weren't going to marry him?"

"Derek is delusional."

"Is he a creep, too?"

"Look at me. Do I look like the kind of person who would marry a creep?"

"Derek says Katrina's not your real name."

"Is that what Derek says?"

"He says you're real name is Miriam. From Northern England."

"That's what he told you?"

"Is it true?"

She shrugged. "Maybe Miriam isn't my real name, either. And I've never been to Northern England."

"So who are you, really?"

"You ask too many questions. I liked you better

when you were stumbling along behind me trying to look anonymous."

"One more question."

"What is it about Americans? Don't you ever shut up?"

"My wife asks me the same question."

"Don't tell me someone was crazy enough to marry you?"

"Can I ask a question or not?"

"If you promise to keep quiet afterwards."

"Fair enough. Where are we going?"

She gave him a sideways glance. "Come on, you're not really married, are you?"

"Why does that surprise you?"

"A tough guy gangster who goes home to his wife and kids. Or do you have kids?

"I might have kids," Tree conceded.

"Boy, you must be some father."

"Just tell me where we're going, will you?"

"A little sensitive, are we?"

"Not at all."

"I've got you on the ropes, I like that," she said with satisfaction. "Where are we going? Where do you think we're going?"

"That's what I want you to tell me."

"Well, too bad," she said. "You're just going to have to wait and see."

13

London streets dark, then brightly lit, alive with commercial establishments, then cast in leafy residential silence; streets so narrow Tree was amazed she could thread through them into wide thoroughfares all but empty at that time of the night.

Along the way, Tree noted the absence of stop signs. Or, else Katrina ignored them. She drove like—no other word for it—a maniac, long slim legs alternately pumping the clutch and the brake pedal, her left hand moving ceaselessly through the gears. A woman—an armed woman at that—in a mini skirt and décolletage, the light shifting around her. He tried not to think where she was taking him. He tried not to think about anything.

Katrina slowed the Land Rover, and Tree realized with a start that they were swinging onto Golborne Road and the dark mass of Trellick Tower. "This is where you live," he said.

She didn't say anything but drove past to a roundabout that put her onto Elkstone. She followed it uphill to Great Western Road, crossing the bridge over the canal before making a quick right onto a side street beside the Union Tavern. She shut off the motor off and turned to him. "Let's get this over with."

"Get what over with?"

"You don't know where you are?" The usual disdain with which she inspected him had been replaced by suspicion.

Okay, he was supposed to know where he was. Instead of answering, he unlatched the passenger door and got out.

He allowed her to go ahead into the tavern. Why was he supposed to know about this place? He wondered.

The interior at this time of night was nearly deserted. Katrina crossed the floor to a flight of stairs. Tree followed her down to the quay where picnic tables overlooked the canal and fortress-like apartment blocks across the way.

Few of the tables were occupied. A lone individual sat nursing a beer at the far end. A jolly red-cheeked fellow, a trimmed white beard beneath a wide-brimmed white Borsalino fedora—a debonair Santa Claus dressed in black. He turned twinkly, appreciative eyes toward Katrina as she approached. "There you are, darling," he said. "I was just beginning to wonder where you were."

"Bit of a delay, Leo, nothing to worry about," she said, seating herself on the bench across from him.

"That's reassuring, darling. You know, I do worry about you."

"Seems everyone I meet today is worried about me."

"Is that a fact?" Leo said.

"It turns out you don't have to worry, not with this bloke trailing me around."

Tree's heart beat fast as the bearded man's gaze, far less admiring, raked him.

"You know my guardian angel, of course," Katrina said.

14

"Yes," Leo Skeleton said in a softly-modulated, mid-Atlantic tone. He flicked another uninterested glance in Tree's direction before his gaze returned to Katrina. "Tell me about this delay."

"Trouble with Derek, that's all. Nothing I couldn't handle."

"Derek." Leo shook his fine head slightly. "I'm getting very tired of his interference. What are we to do about that boy?"

"It's nothing," Karina said. "Don't worry about Derek."

"Increasingly, I must concern myself with him."

"Look, I had a very successful day," Katrina said brightly. "All our friends co-operated."

"You collected everything?"

In response, she opened her shoulder bag and withdrew three envelopes and placed them on the table in front of Leo. He raised his eyebrows. She delved back into her bag and produced three more. The eyebrows made their way back down to where his eyes had once again become appreciative. There was the hint of a smile.

"Very good. Nicely done. I'm impressed. But then I thought I would be."

"So then why the lack of trust?" Katrina said.

Leo looked confused. "Lack of trust? I'm afraid I have no idea what you're talking about, darling."

Tree's heart thumped louder, a sound he was certain everyone in the Grand Union Tavern could hear.

Katrina jerked a thumb in his direction. "Then why did you send John Rio here to follow me?"

Leo's eyes widened in disbelief quickly undercut by a knowing smile. "Oh, no, my darling, this is your boy. Not mine. I thought you brought him along for protection. Unnecessary, but I am happy to overlook it."

Katrina turned hard eyes on Tree, anger rising in her voice. "He's certainly not my boy. You sent him. He's got nothing to do with me."

"My darling," Leo said reasonably, "why would I send anyone? We had an arrangement. I was certain you would live up to it."

Katrina's gaze hardened even more as it focused on Tree. "Who the hell are you?"

Tree's head hurt. His mind was a blur. Who was he? Katrina was rising to her feet. Leo's face had become stone. "What's going on here?"

Out of the corner of his eye, Tree saw two men shaped like refrigerators he had not previously noticed, get up from a nearby table, showing off de rigueur tattooed forearms. Leo's goons, rising, shaved heads glistening. They looked as though they came from the same British thug factory that produced Todd and Ronnie. Tree wondered why the factory couldn't change the template a bit so that all the tough guys of the world didn't have tattooed arms and shaved heads.

"These guys look like a couple I met earlier today,"

Tree said, trying to keep his voice calm. "Ronnie and Todd. Any relation?"

"Albert and Oliver are what you might call my security professionals," Leo said. "No relation to Ronnie and Todd, although I suppose there is a certain resemblance."

"Careful, Leo," Tree said in the best John Rio voice he could muster under the circumstances. "You don't want them to get too close."

Leo smiled. "No? What happens if they do, darling?"

"It's up to you, but it's not going to be pleasant."

"Well, I'm all for avoiding unpleasantness," Leo said calmly. "So why don't you tell me who you are, and what you think you're doing here."

"The less you know about me, the better," Tree said. "All you really need to know for the moment is that I'm from Scotland Yard." The words were out of Tree's mouth before he quite realized it. He had a moment to try to think from what panicky depths they might have emerged before Leo burst out laughing.

"And I'm a monkey's uncle," he pronounced. "Darling, you may be many things, but a Scotland Yard man is almost certainly not one of them."

But Tree noticed that the tattooed refrigerators had stopped their march toward him. Katrina remained on her feet, but now a slightly quizzical expression marred her perfect features.

"I'm not on the force if that's what you're getting at," Tree hurriedly amended. "Let's say they've got me in a position where it's necessary to do a job for them."

"What kind of job would that be?"

"Nothing to do with any of you—at least until now," Tree said.

"What are you getting at?" The look of amusement had evaporated from Leo's rosy face. His eyes had become blazing slits of doubt.

Tree, feeling a lot more confident than he should, sauntered over to Leo's table and sat down on the bench next to him, forcing Leo to twist around his large head in order to keep eyes on Tree. Taking a deep breath, Tree said, "I'm an American, working over here with Hale Stayner for the past couple of years."

"Derek's father?" Katrina managed to sound surprised and disbelieving at the same time.

"Yes, that's right," Tree said. "I was working for Hale when the lads from Scotland Yard fraud squad took me out one night for a beer and informed me that they were investigating my boss. If I didn't co-operate, I would be arrested and charged in connection with his Ponzi scheme."

"Hale was running a Ponzi scheme?"

"That's what Scotland Yard alleges. They needed more proof, though. That's where I came in." Tree was on a roll now. "They said I could poke around without arousing suspicion." He looked at Katrina. "When you cancelled your marriage to Derek, alarm bells went off at the Yard. They wanted to know more about you. They figured I could tell them. Well, I didn't know anything, but that's not what they wanted to hear. So I started following you."

"And here you are—exactly where you shouldn't

be." Leo's accompanying smile was decidedly unfriend-ly.

"Into something I hadn't expected," Tree added.

That caused Leo's eyebrows to shoot up. "But my darling, what makes you think there is anything?"

"Why don't I walk out of here and talk to my minders at the Yard about what I've seen, and let them decide?"

The muscles around Katrina's mouth tightened, but she didn't say anything. Leo let out his breath. In a low, gentle voice, he said, "What is it you want?"

"Money, of course," Tree said. "Cut me in on this, make me part of it."

"In exchange for your silence?"

"If I'm getting paid to be quiet, I would be a fool to say anything, wouldn't I?"

"You are a fool for playing at this," Leo said.

Tree's heart once again began performing its disconcerting jungle drum beat. "Am I?"

Instead of answering immediately, Leo traded a quick glance with Katrina. Then he shrugged, and seemed to notice his glass of beer. "Look at that. Wasting a perfectly good Lager in pursuit of a conversation that isn't getting us anywhere."

Tree thought Leo would pick up the beer, but he didn't. Instead, he addressed Tree. "Here's what you're going to do," he said. "Katrina is going to take you back to her place. It's just around the corner."

"I know where it is," Tree said.

"You can have a drink there, something to eat. Relax a while."

"Why would I do that?" Tree demanded.

"Because I need time to check with my sources," Leo said.

"I doubt your sources will be able to tell you anything," Tree said, perhaps a little too hurriedly. "This operation is being run under the radar."

Leo responded by waving a dismissive hand. "If everything's on the up and up, then I'll visit around midnight and you'll be recompensed for your time—and your cooperation with us."

"I don't like this at all," Katrina said.

"No one's asking you," he snapped. "Particularly since it's your carelessness that has brought us to this point. Take him back to the apartment. Wait for me there. If he gives you any trouble, use that gun you're always carrying around, and shoot him."

"Don't I have anything to say about this?" Tree interjected.

Leo shot a glare in his direction. "Not a damn thing, darling. Go with Katrina and thank your lucky stars these gentlemen behind you don't drown you in the canal."

Tree glanced at the tattooed goons. They looked as though they would like to do exactly that.

15

They got as far as the sidewalk outside the Grand Union Tavern when a voice called, "Katrina."

They both turned to see Leo framed in the doorway. "A word if I might."

Katrina went back to him. Tree watched her listen and nod as Leo spoke. Then Leo was gone and Katrina returned to Tree. "What was that all about?"

"Let's get going," Katrina said.

They walked around to where she had parked her Land Rover. He stopped her as she was about to get in. "Tell me what you and Leo were talking about."

"You," she said.

"Me?" Tree said, trying to sound nonchalant. "What were you saying?"

"Leo suggested I seduce you." Katrina said it the same way she would say that Leo had suggested she pick up a snack on the way to the apartment. She got in the vehicle.

"I can't wait to hear what you said about that," he said.

"I'll just bet," Katrina said. She got inside the Land Rover and closed the door.

Tree went around and by the time he got in she had started the engine. He attached his seatbelt and she started the vehicle forward.

"I told him that I didn't think it was necessary," she said matter-of-factly, swinging the wheel around.

"Oh, yeah? And why is that?"

"Why is it not necessary to seduce you? Because I've already done it."

"You seduced me?"

"Don't you think I have?"

"No, I don't," Tree said adamantly.

"Are you kidding? You're following me around like a lost puppy. You're seduced, take it from me."

"I'm old enough to be your father." Did he sound defensive? Yes, he did.

"You think that makes any difference?"

"And I'm happily married," Tree added.

Katrina just laughed. "American John Rio, the happily-married geezer who follows me around all day yet claims he isn't seduced? You are some piece of work."

"Is geezer better than being a creep?"

"Marginally. Don't worry, I'm not going to seduce you. You're safe with me."

"That's a relief," Tree said.

"So why don't you tell me what it is you're really up to."

"It's just like I told Leo," Tree said.

"You lied to me, why do I suspect you lied to Leo, too."

"I didn't so much lie as go along with you."

"That's what they call a lie."

"I couldn't very well tell you I was working for Scotland Yard, could I? Besides, what about you, Ka-

trina? Or is it, Katrina? I'm with someone and I'm not
even sure what her name is."

"Maybe I've fooled you, John Rio—if that's *your*
real name. Maybe the lie is that there is no lie at all.
Maybe I'm exactly what I say I am—which is more
than I can probably say about you."

That was true enough, Tree thought.

She continued, "Real or false, the names don't
make much difference. Whoever I am, I'm like everyone else. I want my share of the prize. That's what all
this is about, yeah?"

"You don't think you're better than that?"

"What are you trying to do? Save me? Is that it?"

"Maybe I see a better you," Tree said.

"Before you get too judgmental, better take a close
look in a mirror."

"Fair enough," Tree said. Better to shut up and remember he was tough, duplicitous John Rio, not Tree
Callister trying to help a young woman—a woman who
didn't appear to want help.

Katrina concentrated on turning the Land Rover
onto Elkstone past Meanwhile Gardens and then onto
Golborne Road where, as usual, dozens of men stood
in the yellowy light thrown off by the café next door to
Trellick Tower. The men talked and laughed together,
smoking, drinking sodas, taking little notice of the vehicle parking across the street or of the two strangers
hurrying together into the apartment complex.

Tree's mind swirled with various scenarios he
might play out. If he told Katrina who he really was
that would only get him into more trouble than he was

in right now, not that she would believe him, anyway. No, for now he was John Rio, undercover operative for Scotland Yard.

And the night was not over.

Katrina used her key fob to buzz into the lobby. The security guard manning the front desk—it was too much to call him a concierge—was preoccupied talking into his telephone-headset in a language Tree didn't recognize.

Four people waited at the elevators: a young couple dressed in identical Arsenal football jerseys; a grandmother type wearing a black hijab fussing over a carriage containing a sleeping infant; a young guy in T-shirt and jeans tapping impatiently at his smart phone screen.

When the elevator doors opened, Tree half expected Freddie to step out, reacting with alarm at the sudden appearance of her husband, giving everything away. But the inside of the elevator was empty. Tree heaved a silent sigh of relief. Whatever was to happen, he didn't want his wife involved.

Katrina went ahead of him onto the elevator, dodging the grandmother in the hijab pushing the carriage. The young guy, smart phone still in hand, barged on as though this was the last elevator of the night. The two Arsenal fans sauntered on last as the polite electronic voice announced the doors were closing.

By the time the elevator reached the thirtieth floor all the other passengers had left. Katrina and Tree were alone. She turned to look at him. "What's the matter with you?"

"I'm fine," Tree said.

"You look nervous."

"Not me," Tree said, lying through his teeth.

"You've got nothing to worry about," she said as the elevator came to a stop. "Or maybe everything," she added, stepping into the corridor.

They went through the fire doors and along a passageway, Tree trying to ignore the dazzling view of central London at night and the distant, glowing office tower known with varying degrees of horror and admiration as the Shard.

Katrina stopped at the end of the passage and unlocked the door. Tree followed her into an interior similar in layout to the apartment he and Freddie occupied.

Katrina threw her shoulder bag onto a sofa in the sparsely furnished sitting room. The view out the sliding glass doors was obstructed by the middle-aged man who stood on the balcony tossing away a cigarette. When he saw Katrina with Tree, the man frowned and then came through the door into the living room. Balding, with icy blue eyes glaring out like pale searchlights from a face the color of porridge, nondescript tie askew, white shirt open at the collar, trailing the stale smell of too many cigarettes.

"There you are, Katrina," he said. "And I see you've brought a friend."

"He's no friend of mine," said Katrina grimly. "He's one of yours."

"One of mine?" The man looked bemused. "What is he then? A fellow member of the Caucasian race?"

"Pricks Unlimited. A growing club around here," Katrina said.

The porridge-face man gave her a blank look.

"He works for you. Works for Scotland Yard," Katrina said.

The man looked less amused. "What's this? I'm not following."

Katrina said, "I picked him up this afternoon. Derek and his people tried to kidnap us."

"Kidnap you?" Now the man looked alarmed.

"They grabbed this bloke at the same time as they grabbed me. I thought Leo had sent him. But it turns out he's working for you lot."

The porridge-face man moved toward Tree, head lifted, as if to sniff at something unknown and faintly distasteful. "What's this? Scotland Yard, you say?"

"Like I told Katrina and Leo, I'm not Scotland Yard." Tree spoke quickly, attempting to keep the renewed onset of panic out of his voice, trying to be John Rio, the tough guy who could handle any situation. "However, I am doing some work for them."

"Yeah?" The porridge face filled with the same suspicion Tree had been seeing all day. "What kind of work might that be?"

Now it was Tree's turn to feign the narrowing of his eyes: John Rio showing his own sense of doubt. "Who are you, pal?" he demanded. "And why should I tell you anything?"

Katrina issued an unexpected snort of laughter. "Better tell him, Alec."

"Detective Commander Alec Mackenzie," the porridge-face man said in the sort of commanding voice Tree usually heard moments before being arrested.

Katrina said with a sneer, "That's Alec all right, copper through and through, yeah." For the first time that evening, she actually seemed to be enjoying herself.

"Tell you what I'd like you to do, mate," Mackenzie said. "I'd like you to take a couple of steps back, turn around, spread your legs, and then palms out, press your hands against the wall."

"I don't know why I should do that." The voice of John Rio again, albeit a trifle more jittery than he should sound.

The words were barely out of his mouth before three young men with close-cropped hair and smooth faces unmarked by the ravages of age, materialized from another room. "I'm sure you want to co-operate with us, mate, but just in case you don't..." Mackenzie allowed the sentence to tail off with a nod to the newcomers.

Without further objection, Tree turned, spread his legs and pressed his raised hands against the wall. One of the young officers moved in and patted him down. "He's got nothing, except keys and an Oyster card."

"All right," Mackenzie said. "You can turn around now."

Tree did as he was told. Mackenzie had the Oyster card and set of keys in his hand. He held up the Trellick Tower entry fob. "This gets you into the building."

"That's right," Tree said. "I live in the building."

"You *live* here?" Katrina was at Mackenzie's elbow. The pleasurable look on her face was gone.

"For the time being, yes. I knew you were here. I'd seen a photograph. When I saw you at the Golborne Deli this morning, I decided to follow you."

"Why the hell would you do that?"

"My name's not John Rio," Tree said.

Katrina looked exasperated. "Have you spoken one true word since we met?"

"As many truthful words as you have," he replied.

"Okay, okay," Mackenzie interjected. "So give us the latest version of your truth, mate."

"My name is Tree Callister. I'm married to Freddie Stayner, Derek Stayner's aunt."

"Derek?" Katrina said, sounding more confused than ever.

"Katrina's fiancé?" Mackenzie also sounded confused.

"He's not my fiancé," Katrina insisted.

"My wife and I are here for your wedding."

"There isn't going to be a wedding." Katrina sounded more agitated than ever.

"I know that," Tree said.

"I don't understand," Mackenzie said. "What's any of this got to do with deciding to trail around after Katrina?"

"My brother in law said he didn't know much about Katrina. She had cancelled the wedding, and then, suddenly, there she was buying coffee at the Golborne Deli." He shrugged. "It was a stupid idea that got out of hand."

Katrina angrily shook her head and turned to Mackenzie. "This is crazy. He's lying. He's working for you people, and he tried to blackmail Leo to keep quiet. That's why Leo's going to arrive any moment now. If we keep this up, it's going to blow everything."

"What are you all up to?" Tree demanded.

Nobody spoke. Katrina finally took Mackenzie's arm and said, "No matter how he got here, or who he really is, for the moment, he's John Rio, and Leo is expecting him to be here."

"What does Leo want with him?" asked Mackenzie.

Katrina said, "Leo probably wants to kill him."

16

"I don't want Leo killing me," Tree managed to say. Katrina gave him a look. "I don't know, after what you've put me through today, maybe it's not such a bad idea."

"Tell me what's supposed to happen," Mackenzie said.

"I was to bring him here, keep him occupied, and then take him for a walk in Meanwhile Gardens." Katrina's expression was blank as she spoke.

"And what was supposed to happen then?"

"Let's just say Leo is not a fellow who is going to put up with some lowlife police informant trying to blackmail him."

Mackenzie gave Tree a hard look. "Is that what you are trying to do?"

"I'm trying to save my skin," Tree said.

"Let's talk out on the balcony," he said to Tree.

"What do you want to talk to him about?" demanded Katrina.

"A couple of words in private, that's all," Mackenzie said.

"I don't like this," Katrina said.

"Besides, I need a ciggy," Mackenzie said, walking over to the glass door and sliding it open. He and Tree stepped onto the balcony. A cooling breeze ruffled Mackenzie's thinning hair as he leaned against the railing. Tree shivered. He couldn't tell whether it was the night air or fear. He doubted it was the air.

"Close that door, will you?" Tree did as he was asked. "There's the lad. Care for a cigarette?"

"No thanks," Tree said.

Mackenzie produced a package of Marlboros. "Filthy habit, of course." That didn't stop him from extracting a cigarette, sticking it in his mouth, and lighting up. The cigarette had the effect of making his porridge face even less attractive. He blew smoke into the air. "That's better," he said. He took another puff while giving Tree the once over. "The point is, mate, I believe you."

"Believe what?" Tree asked.

"Believe that you're working for us coppers. I mean that stuff about the wedding, clever, quick thinking. But of course you're with us. Makes sense. I'm not aware of the operation you're involved in, but then all sorts of stuff is going down without the right hand knowing what the left is up to."

"I'm *not* working for the Yard," Tree insisted. "That was a lie. My name is Tree Callister, like I said. I'm here for a wedding. I did something stupid and got myself involved in things I shouldn't be involved in."

Mackenzie gave him a wink. "Play it any way you want. Fine by me." He blew more smoke into the air before he said, "As long as you take the walk in Meanwhile Gardens."

"What?" Tree said.

"You heard me."

"I don't think that's a good idea."

"If you want to get out of the mess you are in—and believe me, no matter who you are, you are in trouble—then go for a walk. We will be right there to protect you. Don't worry."

"Don't worry?" Tree said. "You stake me out in the jungle and you tell me not to worry? I'm not going to do it."

"Then there's Katrina," Mackenzie said.

"What about her?"

"This doesn't work out the way it's supposed to, she's on her way to a long stint at Bronzefield."

"Bronzefield? What's Bronzefield?"

"Largest women's prison in Europe. Believe me, you don't want her to end up in there."

"So if I don't go along with this craziness, you arrest her, is that it?"

"She's already under arrest. Question is whether we drop the charges or not. Things work out the way I think they will tonight, she's free and clear—thanks to you."

Mackenzie straightened, tossing what was left of his cigarette over the railing. He grinned at Tree. "You're with London's finest, mate, like I said, not to worry."

Tree tried to swallow. He couldn't do it.

17

Tree insisted he be allowed to use the bathroom. After relieving himself, feeling somewhat better, he ran water into the sink. As he did, he caught his reflection in the wall mirror. A drawn, unshaven face stared back at him. John Rio, tough guy? No, just scared Tree Callister, trying to figure out how he got himself into this jam. More to the point, how was he going to get himself out?

Tough John Rio didn't have the answer to that question. Neither did scared Tree Callister.

He splashed water on his face and that revived him somewhat. But he was tired and hungry, and his head still hurt from the thumping received earlier. He used the towel on a nearby rack to dry his hands and face, wondering about Freddie and what she might be thinking right now. Not that there was much that she could do.

Or was there?

He took several deep breaths, told the image in the mirror that maybe there was a way out of this after all. If only he had the nerve to do what had to be done. The image in the mirror stared back at him doubtfully. He could hardly blame the image.

He took another deep breath, opened the bathroom door, and stepped out to encounter one of the young officers. The cop gave a deadpan stare before moving aside so Tree could pass.

In the living room, Mackenzie hugged Katrina and said, "This is going to work out fine, luv. We'll be right there to make sure nothing happens to you."

"What about me?" Tree announced.

They all turned and looked at him like he was crazy. Mackenzie said, "Smile and look pretty, and hopefully you get out of this alive."

"That's not very reassuring," Tree said.

"Here's what's reassuring," Mackenzie said. "We have people positioned in the park, okay? All you have to do is go outside, and take a stroll."

"Where are you going to be?"

"I won't be far away. Not to worry."

"You keep saying that," Tree said.

Mackenzie turned to Katrina. "All set?" Katrina nodded. "All right, then, off you go."

Tree followed Katrina along the passageway, through the fire doors to the elevators in the blue-tiled foyer. Katrina pressed the down button and a moment later the elevator doors swished open accompanied by the usual reassuring announcement that the doors were, in fact, opening.

They stepped inside, and the doors hushed shut. Tree pressed against the bar running horizontally along the wall. He looked at Katrina. "They aren't really cops, are they?"

"Just do what you're supposed to do," she answered. "That's all you have to worry about right now."

The elevator came to a stop. Katrina looked confused. "What are you doing?"

"What are you talking about?"

"Why are we stopping?" She looked at him accusingly.

Before Tree had to answer, the announcement came that the doors were opening. As soon as that happened, Tree punched Katrina in the face. She flew back against the wall, and as she did, he seized her and threw her out the open doors, grabbing at her shoulder bag as she was propelled forward.

Katrina landed with a hard thud on the floor outside the elevator, long legs sprawling. Tree came out holding her shoulder bag, fumbling to get it open as Katrina began to rally. Her heels slipped on the floor as she tried to rise to her feet, blood dripping from her nose. Tree got the bag open.

Katrina was on her feet shouting incoherently, face twisted, flawless beauty replaced by a fine imitation of a feral creature about to attack. He found the gun he was looking for, yanked it out of the bag, and pointed it at her.

When Katrina saw her own gun in the wrong hand, it brought her to a stop, breathing heavily, nose bleeding hair in disarray.

"Let me have my bag—there's a tissue."

He threw her the bag. She caught it, leaned back against the wall, and fished out a wad of tissues. She pressed several against her nose. "Very stupid move," she said with surprising composure.

"Go through those fire doors," Tree ordered, very

much Tough John Rio for the moment. Amazing how nasty you could get with a gun in your hand.

"What are you going to do, shoot me?"

"I'm an American," Tree said. "That's what we do. We have guns; we shoot people. Now go through the doors."

"What do you think you're going to accomplish?"

"Just do it," Tree said.

She hesitated and then slowly turned and, still holding the tissues against her bleeding nose, stumbled forward. He followed her along the hall. When they got to apartment one-eighty-four, he told her to stop. He pounded on the door. "Freddie," he called. "Open up."

18

Tree knocked again. "Freddie, it's me. Open the door."

From behind the door the sound of shuffling and then the click of turning locks. Finally, the door opened a crack. A voice said, "Tree?"

"Freddie, let me in," Tree said.

The door opened wider. A tousled, sleepy Freddie in pajamas said, "Good grief."

Tree pushed Katrina into the apartment. He followed behind her, closing the door. "Lock it."

Freddie moved to turn the lock. She turned, with widening eyes inspecting the gun and then the girl it was being pointed at.

"I keep swearing I'm not going to ask you what's going on," Freddie said. "So I'm going to ask you: what the *hell* is going on?"

"Who's this?" Katrina demanded.

Freddie trained a hostile gaze at Katrina saying, "Who are you?"

"She's Derek's fiancée," Tree said. "Katrina, meet Fredryka Stayner."

"You're Hale's sister?" Katrina said.

"I thought you looked familiar," Freddie said. She addressed Tree. "What's she doing here, and why do you have a gun?"

"It's a long story," Tree said.

"You travel thousands of miles to a foreign country where no one has a gun, and somehow you end up with a gun?"

Tree said, "Let's go into the other room and sit down."

Katrina looked as though she was about to object, then thought better of it and moved into the living room where she collapsed onto the sofa.

"Who are you people, anyway?" she said.

"A couple of your wedding guests," Tree said.

Katrina rolled her eyes. "I don't believe it."

"It's true," chimed in Freddie. "Who do you think we are?"

Katrina nodded at Tree. "He's an American hood named John Rio who's managed to make my life a total misery."

"Well, he's American all right," Freddie said. "But his name's not John Rio, and I'm afraid he's not much of a hood."

"No? Then what's he doing with that gun?"

Freddie looked at Tree. "Good question, Tree. Where did you get that gun?"

"It belongs to Katrina," Tree said.

"He stole it from me after he punched me in the nose," Katrina said.

"Tree?" Freddie said in an astonished voice. "He punched you?"

"Why do you think I'm bleeding?"

Freddie fixed a fierce glare on her husband. "You didn't hit this young woman did you?"

"I didn't have a lot of choice," Tree said.

"You always have a choice," Freddie declared. "You have a choice *not* to hit a woman."

"I couldn't agree more," Katrina said.

"Tree, I want you to put that gun away," Freddie said in a stern voice. "I don't like you with a gun. It makes me very nervous."

Tree looked at Katrina. "What about it? Can I put the gun away?"

"I want it back," she said.

"I don't think so," Tree said.

"Tree, please give me the gun," Freddie ordered.

"I hope this isn't going to turn out to be a mistake," Tree said, handing her the gun, stock first. Freddie held it gingerly in her fingers and then carried it out of the room. She came back a moment later without the gun but with a damp facecloth.

"Here, try this," she said, bending to take the bloody tissue away from Katrina's nose and replace it with the facecloth. "It doesn't look too bad. Bleeding's mostly stopped."

"Thank you," Katrina said grudgingly. She held the washcloth against her nose and studied Freddie. "What is it with you two? I have no idea whether you're telling the truth—"

"My husband tells the truth," said Freddie the loyalist.

"Yeah, well, that's not my experience with him," Katrina said. "But you go ahead and live with whatever fantasy that helps you stay married to this guy. But here's some free advice, lady: get out of here, get out of London. Go back to where you came from and forget you were ever any part of this."

"What is it we're a part of?" Tree said.

"Believe me, you already know too much, you don't want to know more," Katrina said.

"I don't know a thing," Freddie said.

Tree slumped down in a chair facing Katrina, exhaustion washing through him. His head was hurting again. He shook off the fatigue and leaned forward. "Here's the thing. I'm dead tired. I've been hit on the head, chased and threatened by various young men with tattoos and called a creep by you."

"A creep who hits women," Katrina amended.

"I've watched you take envelopes from people who obviously don't like giving them to you, and then hand those envelopes over to a character named Leo Skeleton who looks like someone's eccentric grandfather but appears to be a notorious London gangster. From what I can see, you and Leo and possibly Derek, too, have been involved in some sort of blackmailing scheme."

Katrina did not respond but continued to hold the facecloth against her nose.

"Now I've encountered cops who, instead of protecting me, and arresting you, seem as anxious as Leo to get me killed. Like I told you before, I don't think those characters up there *are* police, so right now I'm inclined to phone the people who are and let them deal with all this."

"I wouldn't call the police," Katrina said.

"Why not?" chimed in Freddie.

"Because it would put me in a very awkward position," Katrina said.

Freddie said, "If you don't mind my saying so, you already appear to be in a very awkward position."

"No thanks to your husband—who now threatens to make things worse."

"Then tell me what's going on," Tree said. "No lies. Straight goods."

"No lies? Well, that's a change isn't it?" Katrina, glanced at Freddie hovering in the background, and then gingerly removed the facecloth from her nose, sniffed a bit, unsure it wouldn't start bleeding again. Reassured, she sat back. "I guess I could try it without the lies. A different experience, kind of weird, I suppose. But I could try."

"Please do."

Katrina shifted around, touching tentatively at her jaw. Freddie said, "You're turning black and blue, Katrina. Let me see if I can find some ice to put on that."

"Thanks. Much appreciated." Katrina aimed a fleeting smile at Freddie. "You're not a bad person considering who your husband is."

"Don't be too hard on Tree," Freddie said. "He sort of grows on you after a while."

"You must be a saint," Katrina said.

"Let's get back on track," Tree said. "Is this some sort of blackmail scheme you're involved in?"

She nodded. "Leo Skeleton is very good at getting information about people."

"Presumably very important people," Tree said.

"No one blackmails unimportant people, do they?

Unimportant people don't have money. Powerful people do. Politicians, businessmen, lesser members of Royalty, wallowing in the stuff."

"Leo was able to collect dirt on them."

"Powerful people have a habit of behaving badly. They should know better by now, but they don't. They do the sort of things the tabloids here live on; things these people would keep out of the papers at just about any cost."

"Did Leo have anything to do with the revelations about Lord Justin Butler that I've been reading about?"

"Butler refused to pay Leo off."

"So after Bad Butler's indiscretions got into the papers, everyone understood it was better to pay," Tree said.

Katrina nodded. "You saw some of the results today. Anyone who was hesitant or trying to delay suddenly became very cooperative. As you might imagine, all this has been in the planning stage for a long time."

"Was it in the plan for Lord Butler to commit suicide."

Katrina lowered her eyes. "No, of course not."

"How did you become involved?"

"Derek. His father had cut him off, another business he invested in had gone bad and he was deeply in debt. Derek knew a fellow named Martin Bennett. Marty really did play on the dark side, knew some of London's most notorious bent boys—more to the point, he knew Leo, and that's how we became involved with him."

"Bent boys," Tree said. "You mean gangsters."

"Real bastards, yeah?"

"So how did you fit into all this?"

"They needed a go-between, someone to interact with the marks, convince them or their people we had their best interests at heart. They thought I would be ideal for the job."

"And were you?" Freddie asked. "Ideal for the job, I mean."

"I suppose I was." She shrugged.

"I don't understand," Tree said. "If you and Derek were working together. Why would he kidnap you?"

"You mean why would he *try* to kidnap me?"

"Yes, all right," Tree said.

"I was no longer with him. No longer *wanted* to be with him. Derek was doing a lot of drugs, booze, acting crazier and crazier. Leo was getting pretty fed up. Derek and Marty fought with Leo. The next thing, Marty's body shows up in the shrubbery in Meanwhile Gardens, and Leo's on my doorstep telling me that Derek's liable to be next if he doesn't smarten up, and if I know what's good for me, I'd better stick with Leo."

"So you switched sides?"

"I didn't think there was a lot of choice. Anyway, that's how the two of us ended up being jumped by Derek's lads, and everything that has happened, started to happen."

Freddie looked at Tree. "You were kidnapped?"

"Briefly," Tree said.

Freddie, astonished: "You just got here. How can you get kidnapped—even briefly?"

"I keep telling you, it's a long story."

"Yes, you do," Freddie said.

"And those people upstairs, who are they?" Tree said to Katrina.

"I know what you're thinking, but they are police. Look, I'm working with these guys, yeah?"

"I'm very confused as to exactly who you're with and who you're not with," Freddie said.

"Can't say I blame you," Katrina said. "I'm a bit confused myself. Let's say certain police officers got wind of what Leo was up to. They gave me a choice. Either I could go to jail or I could help them. Needless to say, I don't want to go to jail, so, here I am."

"In a lot of trouble," Freddie said.

"Yes, I am," Katrina said. "My own fault, I guess, but I was doing a fair job of extracting myself from a very dangerous situation, at least I thought I was, until your husband came along and really cocked things up."

Someone banged on the door.

"Who could that possibly be?" Freddie said.

Tree looked at Katrina. "This is your apartment," she protested. "I have no idea who's out there."

The banging stopped momentarily, and then resumed. Tree looked at Freddie who looked at Katrina. "Quit with the accusing looks," she said. "There's no way anyone upstairs could know I'm here."

"Let me handle this." Freddie swept from the room. Tree jumped up to follow her starting to say something about not unlocking the door as Freddie unlocked the door.

The police weren't standing there. And neither were any gangsters.

But Hale Stayner was.

Freddie said, "Hale. What are you doing here?"

"What do you mean?" Hale said. "You phoned, worried about Tree. I thought I'd better come around and make sure you're all right." He looked over Freddie's shoulder. "But there's Tree. So he hasn't disappeared." Then his eyes popped. "Katrina?"

"Hello, Hale," Katrina said in a dull voice.

Hale's face filled with confusion. "I don't understand. What's going on here?" He addressed Tree. "Freddie called and said you had gone missing. She wondered if I should call the police."

"So what did you do?" Tree said.

Hale said, "I called the police."

As though on cue, the apartment door burst open and the three officers from upstairs were crowding into the room, DC John Mackenzie leading them.

"Somebody called the police," Mackenzie said. He was smiling when he said it.

19

"You *are* a cop," Tree said.

"Yes I am," Mackenzie said. "And I am placing you under arrest."

"What's the charge?" Freddie demanded.

"Who are you?" Mackenzie said.

"I am his wife."

Mackenzie looked crossly at Katrina. "I didn't think you could make this more complicated than you have, but once again I have underestimated you."

"This has nothing to do with me," Katrina protested.

"And who is this gentleman?" Mackenzie scowled in Hale's direction."

"I'm the chap who called the police," Hale said.

"Why would you do that?" Mackenzie demanded.

"Because this man had gone missing." Hale pointed at Tree.

"He's not missing now," Mackenzie said.

"Apparently a false alarm," Hale said.

"This is Derek's father," Katrina managed to interject.

"And I'm his aunt," said Freddie.

"Good God in Heaven," Mackenzie said, sounding a combination of mystification and frustration.

He turned to Tree, his voice becoming angry. "You have become an irritant, Mr. Callister." He pointed an accusatory finger at Katrina. "And as for you, Katrina, as far as I'm concerned you are on your way to jail."

"What are you talking about?" Katrina demanded.

"You have failed miserably to hold up your end of our agreement."

"Listen," Katrina protested, "don't blame me for any of this, yeah? I've co-operated with you people and it all would have worked out—if it wasn't for him." It was her turn to point a finger; hers was in Tree's direction.

"What the devil is going on here?" repeated an even more confused Hale. "What have you been up to, Katrina, that requires you to be working with these officers?"

"Why don't you ask your son?" she said sullenly.

"What's that mean? What's my son got to do with any of this?"

"Your son isn't what you think he is, put it that way."

"If you've gotten Derek into trouble with your antics, so help me—"

"What kind of balls up is this, anyway?" a voice called out.

The apartment door had been left open, allowing Leo to make his entrance, still Santa in a Borsalino, but now in a trench coat. Of course, Tree thought. The English villain of the piece would be wearing a trench coat.

"You got my message," said Mackenzie.

"Indeed," Leo said.

"I told you to wait outside," Mackenzie said.

"I am not the waiting type, darling," Leo said. "The way everything is getting cocked up this evening, I thought I'd best make an appearance."

"Now everybody knows we're in bed with you."

"You're not in bed with me, darling, don't you wish," Leo said, his face twisting in anger as he surveyed the room. "What a bloody mess."

"I thought you were a cop," Tree said to Mackenzie as one of the young officers yanked his hands behind his back.

"They're coppers all right," Leo said. "They're just not very good coppers."

20

Following a fair amount of heated back and forth between Leo and Mackenzie, Leo got on his cellphone and a few minutes later, Mackenzie and his men were replaced by Albert and Oliver, Leo's two shaved and tattooed thugs. They brought duct tape along with them and proceeded to use it to bind Tree's hands behind his back. Then they did the same for Hale and Freddie.

When the two started toward Katrina, she jerked away, calling to Leo, "Hey, what's this about? I'm on your side, remember?"

"Tell you what this is about," Leo said. "This is about what happens when you don't do what you're told. This is about what happens when it turns out you are more trouble than you're worth."

Katrina said, "You bastard."

"Well, you haven't got much right tonight," Leo responded. "But you're right about that. I am in fact a bastard."

He shoved her back onto the sofa. Albert and Oliver pounced, swinging her around, yanking her arms behind her, wrapping the duct tape around her wrists.

Meantime, Leo was walking away into the kitchen on his cellphone again. He talked quietly for a couple of minutes and then came back into the living room.

"All right, lads," he said, closing his phone. "Truck's downstairs, ready to go. Let's get this over with."

Get what over with? Tree cried out to ask the question that could not be asked with duct tape covering his mouth. And would he want the answer?

Probably not.

Leo opened the apartment door so Albert and Oliver could push their four captives into the hall. Freddie gave Tree a wild glance before Oliver shoved her forward along the corridor. They must have made quite a sight, Tree thought, but this late at night, there was no one around to give them a second look.

Any faint hope Tree had that there would be a security guard in the lobby curious as to why four people tied and gagged with duct tape might be led out of Trellick Tower were soon dashed. There was no sign of anyone. The lobby was deserted.

Even the regulars next door at the café had departed. There was a small truck at the curb, the rear doors open, the engine running. Hale went in the back first, then Freddie, and Tree. Finally, the struggling Katrina was lifted up and tossed in the back.

Oliver and Albert spent time arranging their captives in a row on the floor. Finished, they climbed off the truck. Tree saw Leo poke his head inside, nodding approval before the doors slammed closed and the four of them were left in darkness.

From outside, he could hear Leo say, "Get them down to the country place."

"Blimey," one of the thugs said. "All the way down there."

Leo said, "Best place to deal with these matters. Let's get moving."

A couple of moments later, the truck started forward.

The tape covering his mouth made breathing difficult. The truck's rough motion bounced him alternately against Freddie and Katrina, bound and gagged next to him.

Every part of Tree's body was on fire, a familiar feeling given the perils of the detective work he had chosen to pursue, but unexpected during what was supposed to be a vacation trip to London. Was there nowhere in the world where he could stay out of trouble? If there was such a place, it was not London. The search must continue.

That is if he survived, and right now that didn't appear likely.

An hour or so passed—at least by Tree's reckoning it was an hour—before the truck slowed, and began to make lots of turns indicating they were encountering what the English called roundabouts. After another forty-five minutes or so, Tree heard the truck grind to a stop.

They sat for minutes, Tree relieved to have a respite from being thrown around. He no sooner thought this then the truck started forward again. The road became even rougher than before, the passengers thrown against one another with even greater violence.

Then the truck stopped again, and this time didn't move—not a good thing, Tree thought.

Not a good thing at all.

The rear doors slammed open, bathing the bound prisoners in moonlight. Silhouetted figures crowded the opening. Tree was out and thrown onto the ground. Freddie landed beside him with a painful gasp. He rolled over to find Leo looming over him, a malevolent, trench-coated, Borsalino-hatted Santa.

"There you go," he said. "Won't be long now."

"I'm not sure about this, Leo," Tree heard a voice from somewhere in the darkness above him.

"Of course you're not sure," Leo said. "You're trying to decide if you prefer to spend the rest of your life in prison. Right, darling?"

That brought silence. Then Leo's voice again: "Let us get on with it."

One of the tattooed thugs leaned over and lifted Tree to his feet. Then he did the same for Freddie. Tree now saw that Oliver had Katrina and Hale in standing positions. Katrina appeared defiant while Hale looked plain panic-stricken. Tree knew how he felt.

Leo ordered the group forward. In single file, they moved into a moonlit meadow. Across the way, rising against the starry, cloudless sky, Tree could make out the black towers of what looked like a castle. Of course. They were in the English countryside. There had to be a castle nearby.

They trooped uncertainly across the meadow, the light from the moon showing the way to a distant grove of trees.

When they reached the trees, Leo brought the group to a stop. Below, another field, this one narrower, tumbled through moonlight to the edge of a forest and the castle towers more clearly visible beyond.

Leo moved to Katrina and jerked her down on her knees. Then he did the same with Hale. Hale made anguished, muffled sounds through the duct tape covering his mouth. He was ignored. Leo came abreast of Tree. The two men faced one another. Leo's face was expressionless: Santa Claus making his rounds, doing his grim job. No emotion required.

Tree kneed Santa in the groin. Santa howled, crumpling, his Borsalino flying away.

21

Like a shot, Tree was off across the field. Perhaps not quite like a shot, but he was running for dear life. Behind him he heard someone cry out. He expected the cry to be followed by a gunshot, but there was nothing.

He gained what he told himself was the safety of the trees beyond the field. The moonlight did not penetrate the thick foliage, sinking the world into a place of dark fairy tales. Little Red Riding Hood would not be able to see her hand in front of her, and neither could Little Tree Callister.

He smacked against the rough bark of a tree trunk, recoiling, the wind knocked out of him, trying to shake off the sudden, searing pain, choking, prevented by the duct tape from breathing properly. He crashed through underbrush before falling into a clearing. The moon briefly pointed the way forward. Behind, he could hear bodies thrashing towards him.

Then, as abruptly as the woods were there, they were gone, scenery swept away by an unseen stage manager, leaving the bright moon to show the way across a strip of lawn to the walls of the castle.

A castle would mean people, would it not? People still lived in castles, even in this day and age. Didn't they?

He reached the wall, rough chunks of imbedded

stone going on forever. He followed along until he finally rounded a corner and saw the delivery truck, its rear doors open. Good, thought Tree, relief flooding through him. Humans were about even at this early hour. Humans who could call the police. Humans who could rip the duct tape off his mouth and free his wrists and finally give him desperately-needed relief.

The moon had faded; a milky gray morning light revealed a stone entranceway and a thick medieval door left partially open. Tree propelled himself forward through the door into—well, not the great hall he expected, but a dark, vaulted cellar, blackened casks lining either side of the passageway leading to a set of stairs.

Up the stairs to a passageway. He tried to make a sound of alarm through the tape. All he got for his efforts were a few muted moans that he had difficulty hearing let alone anyone else.

The passageway led him into a long banquet hall. Carved ceiling beams, an ebony floor, hanging wall tapestries, a huge fireplace that took up most of a wall, grotesque faces carved into the mantelpiece, faces full of contempt at having such a stupid person in their midst.

An oil painting above the mantel featured three beautiful women of the 1920s. They lounged elegantly, as only the rich could lounge, perhaps awaiting the arrival of Mr. Noel Coward for the weekend. While they waited, the trio languidly studied Tree, lovely women unperturbed at the intrusion of an aging, unshaven

American with his mouth taped and his hands tied, fighting for his life.

Tree pulled his gaze away from his hosts, noticing two iron spikes implanted in the floor of the fireplace cavity. An iron crosspiece supported the bed on which logs were laid for a fire that was never lit. The spikes gave him an idea.

He fell to his knees, shifting around so that he could move his taped wrists against the edge of the spikes. As he did this, he heard a sound.

Somebody coming.

He moved his wrists faster up and down the spike. He thought he could feel its iron edge begin to cut into the tape. Or was his imagination working overtime, hoping against faint hope?

Footsteps thumped toward him, accompanied by heavy breathing—an out-of-shape pursuer. That was good, Tree thought. Then it flickered through his mind that with his hands literally tied behind his back, he wasn't much of a threat even if his pursuer was winded.

Then, abruptly, the duct tape loosened. But now it was too late. Someone had entered the hall. Tree shrank deeper into the cavity, ripping the tape away from his mouth.

The footsteps came forward, interrupted by more heavy breathing. Tree's wrists parted. Instant relief— and fingers touching iron. He looked around and saw a small black shovel leaning against the fireplace wall. His fingers closed around its handle.

Tree heaved himself out of the cavity, the shovel in

his hand, interrupting a startled Leo, a pale, sweating, disheveled Leo, suffering as much from the chase as Tree, Santa without his Borsalino, revealing thin wisps of white hair.

Except he had a gun.

Tree hit Leo on the side of the head with the shovel. He grunted and reeled back, trying to stay upright, gun hand swinging wildly. Tree hit him again. The gun went off and for a moment Tree was certain he had been shot. But then Leo sagged to his knees, dropping the gun, and Tree saw the blood pouring out of the gash in his forehead, marking the spot where the shovel had done its work.

Bloody Leo lunged, wrapping his arms around Tree's legs. Now it was Tree's turn to fight for his balance. The fight didn't last long. Leo tightened his grip and Tree crashed to the ebony floor. He still had the shovel in his hand, though. He swung it against Leo once, got a reassuring cry of pain out of Santa, and then hit him again and again.

That's when the security guard arrived, an elderly gentleman with a thick mustache, wearing an official-looking cap, his eyes wide with a mixture of fear and amazement. "Here then," he said. "What's all this about?"

Leo had no trouble announcing his version of events: "This man assaulted me," he gasped.

"What in the name of all that's holy are the two of you doing in here assaulting one another?" demanded the security guard. "And what's that on the floor?"

It was a gun, Tree thought dully. Leo's gun, lying

only feet from him. Leo came to a similar realization. He grabbed for it.

Tree kicked at him, and the security guard said, "Here, stop that you two!"

Tree kicked Leo again, receiving another satisfactory groan of pain. Then Tree got hold of the gun. Holding the weapon, he rose shakily to his feet. The security guard now looked genuinely alarmed.

"Here lad," he said nervously. "That's a gun isn't it?"

"It is," Tree said.

"Not every day you see one of those around here, that's a certainty. What do you plan to do with it?"

"I plan to use it to get you to call the local police," Tree said.

"No problem there, lad," replied the security guard. "Glad to oblige."

The guard disappeared, leaving Leo and Tree alone. Leo groaned and rolled onto his back. He lifted himself up by the elbows, trying to get a better look at Tree.

"This is the part where I try to buy you," Leo said.

"This is the part where I say I'm not for sale," Tree replied.

"I thought as much," Leo said. He lay back and for a while was silent. Tree kept the gun trained on his adversary.

"There is the one other thing," Leo said.

"What's that?"

"My suspicion that you won't shoot me."

"I wouldn't count on that," Tree said.

"It's my last hope, really," Leo said. "I'm far too old to go to prison."

"You should have thought of that before now," Tree said.

"You're probably right." Leo lifted himself up by the elbows again. Tree could see the blood streaming down his face. Leo rolled over onto his knees. "Still, might as well give it a try, see what you're made of."

"Just stay where you are," Tree said.

"Bit of a cliché, darling," Leo said. "Try for something more original, will you?"

He started to crawl across the floor, trailing blood behind him.

"Leo, you're not going to make it," Tree said.

"You never know, darling," Leo said. "You never know."

Leo continued to inch away. The security guard, huffing and puffing, hurried back into the room. When he saw Leo, he said "Here now, where the devil do you think you're going?"

"He's trying to make his escape," Tree said.

"Oh, no he isn't," the security guard said. He kicked Leo in the ribs. Leo moaned and fell on his side.

"Police are on their way," the security guard said with satisfaction.

22

Outside the tube station at Piccadilly Circus vendors were handing out copies of the *Evening Standard* . The big black front page headline said, BLACKMAIL RING FOILED: POLITICIANS AND ROYALTY VICTIMS; SCOTLAND YARD DETECTIVES ARRESTED.

Tree grabbed a copy. According to the *Evening Standard*, diligent work by the boys at the Yard had resulted in breaking up of the blackmail ring that had preyed upon London's elite in politics and show business. There were even allegations that members of the Royal family had been subjected to blackmail. In addition to the ring leaders, several police officers who allegedly worked with the gang providing information about the victims, also had been arrested.

The paper said an informant was cooperating with police in their investigation. Tree assumed that the informant was Katrina Phillips. When Leo Skeleton ran after Tree, his two thugs had become nervous and eventually bolted away, leaving Freddie, Hale, and Katrina bound and gagged on the ground. Katrina had managed to wriggle free and disappear. However, she didn't get very far. Police arrested her a few miles away.

"Come along hero of mine," Freddie said, taking his arm. "We're going to be late."

"Some hero," Tree grumbled. "They don't even mention my name in the paper."

"A silent hero," Freddie said. "The best kind."

"I don't like being silent," Tree said. "I'm more than willing to be celebrated across the front pages of the British press."

"I'm sure you are," Freddie said.

They made their way along Piccadilly, choked with theatergoers and tourists, dominated by the iconic LED billboards insistent that Hyundai or Samsung or Coca-Cola brings happiness. "Choose Happiness" was in glowing red letters.

Tree took in the crowds swarming around him, young and very much alive, no inclination to shoot anyone or duct tape mouths or even resort to blackmail. It felt good to be out here with them; it felt so, well, *normal*. So, yes, definitely he would choose happiness. At the end of it all, what else was there? The alternative, as he had been reminded any number of times lately, was death. And that was no choice at all.

"What are you thinking about?" Freddie had taken him by the arm.

"The advice on that billboard up there," Tree said.

"Buy a car?"

"No, choose happiness."

"You need a billboard to figure that out?"

"This is the part of our story where you're supposed to say, 'Oh, darling. Being married to you brings so much happiness.'"

"That's what I'm supposed to say?"

"Words to the effect."

Freddie looked at her husband. "How about this: 'Darling, being married to you gets me in trouble no matter where we go.'"

"There are two schools of thought about that," Tree offered. "The first is that I should never have acted on impulse and followed Katrina."

"The school that I have enrolled in," Freddie said.

"The second school has it that if I had not followed Katrina, the plot to blackmail some of the country's most important politicians, celebrities, and members of the Royal family would never have been exposed."

"Yes," Freddie conceded. "There is that theory."

"But you're not buying into it."

"Let's just say, I prefer that first school that argues you stay out of trouble by not getting into it in the first place."

"I'm beginning to subscribe to that school myself."

"You always say that. But somehow you always end up in trouble. Have you heard any more news about Katrina?"

"It looks as though she is cooperating with the real police of Scotland Yard, or at least the honest ones, so she may escape prosecution. I doubt Derek is going to be so lucky, though."

"Yes, poor Hale, he's devastated by what's happened to his son," Freddie said.

"I wish I had more sympathy for Derek, but it's hard given the fact his goons cracked me over the head and then abducted me."

"You're okay now, so let's relax and try to enjoy what little time we have left in London."

They reached the Gielgud Theater where The *Curious Incident of the Dog in the Night-Time* was playing.

The entranceway was crowded with young people smoking. Freddie made a face. "I hate it when everyone's smoking," she said.

"That's why you should avoid the outdoors," Tree said. "It's where you find the smokers. He looked up at the marquee. "*The Curious Incident of the Dog in the Night-Time*," he said. "I'm really looking forward to this."

"For the last while I've been part of another drama, *The Curious Incident of the Detective in London.*

"Not tonight," Tree said. "Tonight all the drama is on the stage in front of us. All we have to do is sit there."

"I hope so," Freddie said. "With you, I can never be sure."

"Trust me on this," Tree said.

She took his arm and together they started inside. Then she stopped and gazed at him intently. "I love you," she said. "I know we would never have gotten into any of this if it hadn't been for you. But I also know that without you, we would never have gotten out of it."

"I really am a heroic devil, aren't I?"

She gripped him tighter. "Don't get too carried away."

"Not me," he said. "I plan to remain the same humble fellow I've always been."

She gave him a look. They laughed and then together went into the theatre.

Now Available

THE LATEST TREE CALLISTER ADVENTURE

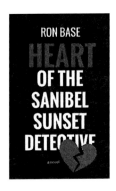

Private Detective Tree Callister is afraid of dying, but that's the least of his problems as he tries to survive the obstacles he encounters when an old friend enlists his help to unravel the truth behind a mysterious list.

Tree is in so much trouble from Sanibel Island to Savannah, Georgia to Washington, D.C. that only his wife, Freddie, can save him!

More information about the new novel at

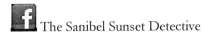 The Sanibel Sunset Detective

ronbase.wordpress.com
ronbase.com
ronbase@ronbase.com

If you enjoyed The Sanibel Sunset Detective
Goes to London…

TURN THE PAGE TO READ AN
EXCERPT FROM

THE SANIBEL SUNSET DETECTIVE

The gripping first novel in Ron Base's bestselling
mystery series

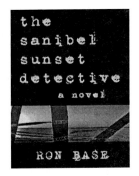

1

The advertisement appeared simultaneously in the Want Ads sections of the Sanibel Island Reporter and the Fort Myers News-Press.

Sanibel Sunset Detective
Professional Investigation
Discretion Guaranteed
1159 Causeway Rd.
Sanibel Island, Fl.
Phone 239-472-2348

A week later, Rex Baxter, president of the Sanibel-Captiva Chamber of Commerce, in what was becoming something of a morning ritual, shambled into Tree Callister's office and presented him with a Starbucks Grande Caffe Latte.

"I'm sick and tired of waiting on you," Rex said.

"What's scary is, I'm starting to look forward to this," Tree said.

"It's not like I feel sorry for you or anything," Rex said. He eased himself into the only empty chair in the tiny office. "You coming to the end of a wasted life with nothing to show for it."

"You've got a point there," Tree said.

Rex was tall with wavy grey hair that made him look like a local TV anchorman, which, in fact, he had been for many years at WBBM-TV in Chicago. Well, not an anchor, exactly. Rex was the weatherman for the station's late afternoon newscast. Before that, he had been a movie actor in 1950s B-pictures. He came to Chicago to host an afternoon movie show. That's how Tree and Rex knew each other. Tree had interviewed him for his newspaper, the Sun-Times. They had been friends ever since.

Originally from Oklahoma, and proud of it, Rex now was almost as much a part of Sanibel as the palm trees and the beaches. Tree, on the other hand, was not part of anything. Tree was an ex-newspaperman who didn't know what to do with himself. Rex let Tree have the office upstairs at the Chamber of Commerce visitors center so he could get started in the detective business. Rex thought Tree was out of his mind, but the office was empty, and it would mean there was another body around to answer the phone when everyone was at lunch.

Rex said, "Okay, try this one on for size. Your favorite private detective movie."

Tree thought about it a moment before he said, "Twilight."

Rex scratched at one of the wattles that had developed beneath his chin. "Twilight? That vampire movie?"

"This is another Twilight. The better Twilight."

"Never even heard of it."

"Paul Newman is an ex-cop, ex-drunk in Los Angeles, living with famous husband-and-wife movie stars played by Gene Hackman and Susan Sarandon. Hackman is Newman's best friend. The scenes between the two of them are priceless. Sort of like us, Rex."

"You're Newman, I'm Hackman, is that it?"

"It's Newman's last starring role. He's too old for it, but he's Paul Newman one final time, a little tired, a little world weary, but not giving into it, beating on, trying to make the best of what he's been handed."

"Like you, Tree."

"Except I'm not Paul Newman. The tragedy of my life. What guy of a certain age doesn't look at Paul Newman on the screen and identify with him? Everyone wants to be Cool Hand Luke."

"What's Twilight about?"

"It's about coming to the end, but if you mean the plot, who knows? If you can remember the plot of a private detective movie, then it's probably not a very good private detective movie."

"Come on," Rex said. "Private detective movies are nothing but plot."

"Oh, yeah? What's The Big Sleep about?"

Rex was silent. "Well, it's about Humphrey Bogart and Lauren Bacall."

Tree grinned. "And that's more than enough plot for any movie. I rest my case."

They were interrupted by the thump of footsteps on the stairs leading to Tree's office. They both turned to see a boy in a Tampa Bay Rays baseball cap appear in the doorway.

"This the Sanibel Sunset Detective Agency?"

"It is indeed," Tree said.

"I want to talk to a detective," the boy said.

Rex winked at Tree and stood. "I've got to get over to the Ding Darling Education Center so I can finish making my gun."

"Your gun?" Tree said.

"A rifle, actually. A replica of the real thing. But it works. Talk to you later."

Rex ambled out past the boy who remained in the doorway. Tree waved at him. "Come on in and have a seat."

The boy ventured tentatively into the room. He was African American. A backpack hung from his shoulders. He wore the usual island uniform: khaki shorts and a T-shirt that was too big for him, with a picture of a fish and "Sanibel Island" printed across the front.

"You are the detective guy?" As though he couldn't quite believe it.

"I wouldn't lie to you," Tree said.

"You don't look like a detective."

"How are detectives supposed to look?"

"Younger," the boy said.

He perched on the edge of the chair vacated by Rex, his head barely visible over the desk.

"So like I could hire you, right?"

"What's your name?"

He hesitated before he said, "Marcello."

"Marcello?"

"Like the Italian actor."

"Marcello Mastroianni?"

The boy shrugged. "My mom said the Italian actor."

"Okay, Marcello. Aren't you a little young to be hiring detectives?"

"How old do you have to be?"

"How old are you?"

Marcello hardly paused before he said, "Twenty-one."

"You shouldn't lie to a detective," Tree said.

"How do you know I'm lying?"

"I'm a detective," he said.

"You think I'm young because you're so old."

Tree looked at him.

"It's my mom," Marcello said.

"What about her?"

"I want you to find her."

"I see. Where is your mom?"

A look of impatience crossed the boy's delicate features. "If I knew that, I wouldn't have to hire you."

"That's true," Tree had to admit.

"I got a card from her," he said.

"Okay."

"Would you like to see it?"

Tree said he would. The boy swung the backpack off his shoulders and from it fished out a small blue greeting card. He handed it to Tree. Fumbling in his shirt pocket, Tree located his glasses and balanced them on the end of his nose. Marcello made a face.

"What are those?"

"The glasses? They're glasses."

"You wear glasses?"

"For reading. Just for reading." Did he sound a tad defensive? He repositioned the glasses on the bridge of his nose and looked at the card. There was a small white heart in the bottom right-hand corner.

Tree opened it up. The handwriting in the interior was neat and feminine.

Hello, my little love,

I know you haven't heard from me for a while, and I'm sorry. I should have written earlier. I love you very much, I want you to know that. I haven't forgotten about you. I think about you all the time. I will be coming for you soon, I promise, darling. In the meantime, please be strong and brave, and remember that you are loved more than you will ever know.

Mommy

Tree handed the card back to Marcello who carefully replaced it in his backpack. Tree took his glasses off and put them back in his shirt pocket. "When did you get this?" he asked.

He looked uneasy. "Can you find my mom or not?"

"Okay, Marcello, it doesn't seem as though she's missing since she recently sent you a letter. She says she's coming to get you and you should be patient."

So what does that mean? You won't find her?"

"If your mom really is missing, you should go to the police."

"I don't like the police."

"Nonetheless, they are the people best equipped to find your mom—if she really is missing."

"What's the use you being a detective and everything if all you do is tell people to call the police?"

"I don't tell that to everyone," Tree said. "Only twelve-year-old boys."

"Well, I'm twenty-one."

"Nonetheless, I think you should go to the police."

The kid got up from the chair. Even then he didn't rise up that much above the desk, Tree noted. A small twelve. Maybe he wasn't even twelve. The boy re-slung the backpack on his shoulders.

"You're old and I don't think I like you," he said.

"Detectives aren't supposed to be liked," said Tree.

"Then you must be a great detective."

Tree couldn't help but smile. He decided to try to be helpful. "Your mother sounds like a nice person, Marcello."

"That's why I want to be with her."

Would you like me to call the police for you?"

Marcello shook his head. "I told you already. I don't like the police."

"That's right. I forgot."

Marcello went out. Tree put his glasses back on, wondering if he should let the boy go. He heard him clomp back down the stairs. Tree swiveled around to stare out the window into the parking lot, still wondering what he should do. Marcello swept past astride a red bicycle. Then he was gone. The kid was from around here, no doubt. He'd be all right. Probably mom and dad were divorced. The boy lived with his father and maybe a stepmother. He missed his real mom, that was all, and then he got that letter, and maybe his mom should have showed up by now and hadn't.

That was it. No more to it than that.

The boy's comments about age irritated him. He wasn't that old, was he? He still had most of his hair and that was a plus, and it had remained mostly black, albeit shot through with grey streaks. He liked to think that just made him more distinguished. He had put on some weight in the last few years, but he worked out three or four times a week and being tall like Rex, six feet, two inches, he was, he believed, able to carry a few extra pounds. Or was he deluding himself? It was the age of delusion. He told himself he did not feel sixty. However sixty was supposed to feel.

In addition to telling himself he did not feel sixty, he also repeated to himself how lucky he was—lucky to have met his wife, Freddie, lucky to have experienced the last great days of Chicago newspapers. He had started out at the Daily News and when that folded, a victim of the world's lack of interest in an afternoon newspaper, he had gone over to the Sun-Times where he toiled away happily. He knew Mike Royko, the legendary Chicago columnist, well, he didn't know Royko, could anyone? But he would nod at Tree when they encountered each other in the city room, and Mike would say, "Hi, there, Tree." A cub of a reporter, barely out of his teens, Tree was thrilled.

Newspapermen—and they were mostly men—wore ties, never fully tied, and white shirts with the collar button undone. They punched at Underwood typewriters with two fingers, and editors yelled "Copy!" and everyone smoked incessantly so that a pall of grey smoke hung constantly over the battlefield that was the city room.

They drank draught beer for lunch at Riccardo's, the watering hole of choice, bitching about the corruption of the Daley political machine that ran Chicago forever—Richard J. Daley, that is, not the son, Richard M. Daley, who, when he was mayor, gentrified the city to the point where Tree barely recognized it. Tree loved all of it, loved it too much, at the expense of things like family.

He loved it so much he hung around long enough to see it all change, which is to say he hung around too long.

His mind drifted to another popular topic lately, the mediocrity of his misspent life. He had a lot of time to ponder that subject. He thought about it in the dispassionate way a man who has recently turned sixty must consider these things. After all, no matter how you cut it, the bulk of a lifetime, its essential weight, already had been mounted on the scale and weighed. The weight in his case was light. The future did not promise much more heft. How could it? There was not, he had to admit, a whole lot of future left to consider. A curious thing to realize that there was more behind you than there was ahead.

He did not think like this out of any sense of depression—Tree could not honestly say he was depressed—more of resignation. This was the way it had turned out, and there was not much he could do about it.

Well, there was one thing. You could open your very own detective agency. Not a universal response to the aging process, but his response. So far it had been pretty quiet. Not unexpected since he had no experience as a detective. Someone asked him how many operatives the Sanibel Sunset Detective Agency employed. Operatives? There was only one operative. W. Tremain Callister—Tree—he was the Sanibel Sunset Detective.

One detective, then, and zero clients. Tree shifted his gaze away from the window.

You could hardly count the kid. Marcello? Probably home by now. Hopefully, someone was giving him a hug and pouring him a glass of milk and he was okay. Probably forgotten all about his visit to a real live private detective.

Except he wasn't much of a detective. Maybe he handled the boy the wrong way. Certainly he was capable of mishandling kids. All you had to do was ask his. Suppose Marcello wasn't home getting a hug and a glass of milk? Suppose someone was knocking him around and his lost mom and that letter were all he had to hang on to? Could his mother really be missing? A lot of kids' parents were missing in action, he supposed. Maybe he should have taken him home and made sure he was all right. He would be fine. Maybe it wasn't even serious. Maybe the kid was playing some sort of weird joke.

Who would be crazy enough to hire Tree Callister, anyway? Paul Newman, sure. He could find your mom and solve your problems because he was Paul Newman. But Tree Callister? What could he ever do for you?

2

Tree left the office late in the afternoon and got into his battered yellow Volkswagen Beetle convertible. His wife Freddie's red Mercedes was at the garage for a tune-up. Tree's job today was to pick her up and drive her home. He was a private investigator. He could handle that.

The traffic heading off the island on Causeway Boulevard was already heavy. He turned on to Periwinkle Way and came along to Dayton's, the late afternoon sun glinting off his windshield, Elvis on the radio singing "Jailhouse Rock." Lately, he had begun listening to one of the local classic rock radio stations for whom time stopped at the end of 1969. He tried to tell himself this had nothing to do with nostalgia for his fading past, but of course it did. "Jailhouse Rock" made him think of the Elvis Presley concert at Cobo Hall in Detroit in 1970, the excitement of seeing a legend who had not performed for ten years, of witnessing a comeback that people still talked about.

Well, people of a certain age still talked about.

Tree supposed his increasing reliance on pop standards also had something to do with his lack of identification with what was happening on contemporary radio. He hated that, hated that the world appeared to be drifting, that what was noise to him was the music of the day to a generation. He was beginning to feel like his parents, the people he swore he would never emulate.

Dayton's Supermarkets had been part of the Fort Myers-Naples-Tampa area since Ray Dayton took over the company after he came back from Vietnam in 1974. Ray's grandfather had started the business on Sanibel in the 1940s. Ray looked more like his grand-dad every day .

Mr. Ray, as he liked to be called, had served his country fighting in Vietnam. Everyone knew that. A sentence containing Mr. Ray's name invariably also carried the information that he was a brave veteran who had been to Nam. That's what everyone said. He had not been to Vietnam. He had been to Nam.

Mr. Ray was talking to Sam Mercer as Tree drove into the parking lot. Sam owned a small resort on Tarpon Bay. He was also president of the Kiwanis Club. Sam and Mr. Ray watched Tree park the Volkswagen. Conversation ceased as he got out of the car and started toward them. Sam removed his sunglasses to get a better look at the interloper. Mr. Ray's short-cropped white hair glistened in the sunlight. His face was like a slab of stone carved out of a windstorm.

"Hey, Tree."

"How are you, Ray?"

Sam said, "How's the detective business, Tree?"

"Busy, busy," Tree said with a smile.

Neither man smiled back. Ray Dayton said, "Freddie's inside, Tree."

"Thanks."

"You should drop around to Kiwanis, Tree." Sam

Mercer spoke slowly, as though addressing someone with learning disabilities. "We could use a detective. Might be good for your business."

"Thanks Sam, I appreciate that."

He could feel their eyes on him as he headed toward Dayton's: the guy's an idiot.

Tree stepped into the supermarket's air conditioned coolness. Freddie appeared in a blur of summer linen hurrying along aisle one (pretzels, chips, beer). Tree tried to imagine her with a pretzel or a beer and couldn't do it. She was on her Blackberry.

"Yes, but Terry any way you look at it, our shrink is too high. We've got to do better. I want a meeting with him. How about tomorrow? Ten o'clock. See you then, Terry."

She got off her phone and her smile brightened. "There you are."

She kissed him quickly on the mouth, a wifely peck, acceptable in public. Tree liked the way she did it. He liked everything about Fredericka Stayner, known to everyone as Freddie—the way she walked, the sweep of her honey-colored hair, the deep green of her eyes, her elegance, the effortless intelligence. Every time he thought of her, it made him smile. After ten years of marriage, he was still smiling.

"The Mercedes isn't going to be ready until tomorrow."

"Then it looks like I'm going to have to drive you home."

"I hate driving in that car," she said. "I wish you'd let me buy a new one."

"It's my pride and joy," Tree said. "The only thing I have in this world."

"You have me," Freddie said.

"Better even than the Beetle," he said, taking her hand.

"I don't rattle, and I'm not constantly blaring old rock and roll tunes."

"I don't listen to old rock all the time," Tree maintained.

"Yes, you do. The next thing you'll try to make me watch The Guns of Navarone again."

"What a lovely way to spend an evening," he said.

She rolled her eyes and squeezed his hand.

Freddie was Tree's fourth wife. He could hardly believe it. Four wives? Impossible. Movie stars married four times. Rock musicians. Not Tree Callister. Years ago, a callow young Chicago reporter, he had interviewed Henry Fonda. As afternoon shadows lengthened across Fonda's still youthfully iconic face, the face of Tom Joad in autumn, the actor expressed anguish over his four marriages. He was ashamed of the divorces. Tree wondered how it was possible to deal with all the emotional and financial complications that many breakups must have entailed.

Now he knew.

He married the first time in his early twenties. What the hell had he been thinking, marrying that young? He wanted the hard-drinking Hemingwayesque newspaper reporter, not a happily married family man. His first wife, Judy, young, dutiful, naïve, desiring all the traditional trappings of marriage, including a husband who came home at night. They produced two children, Raymond and Christopher, before everything fell apart—the bad husband exiting the bad marriage, leaving behind crying children and an angry wife.

Rex Baxter had introduced him to his second wife, Kelly Fleming, a Chicago newscaster who lit up any room she entered. Tree was mesmerized. He remained mesmerized; Kelly less so. A recipe for disaster that ended after three years. Then came Patricia Laine, the entertainment editor at the Sun-Times. She threw him out a little over a year after they married and went off with the editor of the paper, an upgrade.

After Patricia, he was more or less single for the next five years, except for the live-in law student twenty years his junior. The less said about that, the better.

His marriages, he decided, were rites of passage, necessary journeys on the way to destiny in the form of Fredericka Stayner. Not that he believed in destiny—except where Freddie was concerned. That had to be destiny. It could be nothing else.

Friends introduced them at a Gold Coast dinner party. She was a high-powered, hard-driving, department store executive, stunning in Ralph Lauren. As soon as Tree laid eyes on her, he wanted to marry her. That, Freddie said later, was part of his problem. Tree saw a car he liked, he wanted to marry it.

They chatted over pompano and crunchy asparagus. She hadn't seen the Matisse exhibit at the Art Institute of Chicago. Had he? No, hadn't had a chance. Was he even intending to go? he thought to himself. No, but what difference did that make? He suggested they meet the next afternoon. They could look at it together. She delivered what was to be one of many cool, green-eyed appraisals. Green is the rarest eye color, he thought inanely. Where had he read that? He held his breath. She nodded. Two o'clock? Two o'clock would be fine.

He counted the moments until he met her on the steps of the Art Institute. They wandered together through the exhibit, not saying much. Matisse must have been in a particularly slap-dash and simple mood in the period following his return from Morocco but before heading off to the South of France, all the while bemoaning the work that went into his painting. Not only was comedy hard, but according to the never-happy Matisse, so was painting.

Tree marveled at how self-contained Matisse was. His art was all, nothing else existed, not even the world war in progress down the road from his Paris studio. It never seemed to occur to Matisse that the public might not care for his images. What difference did that make? No focus groups in Matisse's world, Tree observed. Freddie laughed and said she didn't much care for this part of Matisse.

They wandered down to American Art Before 1900. Unlike the Matisse exhibit, which was so crowded people jostled for position in front of the paintings, here they were alone except for a bored-looking guard, and even he disappeared after a few minutes.

Nobody gave a hoot about American art before 1900, Tree supposed. Not even for Frederic Remington's stuff which Tree loved because Remington evoked the John Ford westerns he grew up with. Westerns? Freddie groaned. She hated westerns. Who even thought about westerns these days? Tree was willing to forgive her that particular shortcoming. He was willing to forgive her anything. They kissed in front of Remington's "End of the Trail" bronze. Tree kept an eye on the lone Indian warrior astride his horse, head bowed in defeat. Today, he was the warrior victorious, if only briefly. After that, they couldn't stop kissing. They had been kissing ever since.

Freddie had been married twice before. The starter marriage was packaged with all the traditional trimmings: the bride in white, the bridesmaids in pink; the groom and best man in baby-blue tuxedos; the band at the Palmer House reception with featured accordions playing "Welcome to My World." The new husband got too drunk on the wedding night to do anything but throw up in the bridal suite.

The second marriage, as second marriages tend to be, was more serious business. The guy was ten years older, well-to-do, with boutique hotels in Chicago, New York, and Los Angeles. They had a daughter together, Emma. Glenn—that was number two's name—was a controlling drunk who, when things didn't go his way, threatened to kill his wife. Freddie could never be sure if he was serious, but she wasn't taking any chances and got out of the marriage, taking Emma with her.

Tree had to work on Freddie, behave himself in ways he had never before behaved, court her properly, show up when he said he would. None of that was a problem. All the things he could never achieve in his other relationships, were achieved effortlessly with Freddie.

She finally agreed to marry him, commenting that the last thing she expected was to marry some guy who had been married three times before. Not that the two strikes against her were anything to be proud of.

If it was any consolation, Tree said, he never expected to be that guy.

———

Freddie waved at Mr. Ray as they headed toward the car. "I'm meeting Terry at ten tomorrow morning."

"The shrink rate is fine," he called back.

"No it's not," she said. Mr. Ray gave the dead-eyed stare usually reserved for Tree. "Honestly," she said in a low voice, "There are days when I could murder that man."

"Most days I think the Ray Man wants to kill me."

"He continues to believe that all you have to do is pull the trucks up to the back door and unload them."

"But he hired you," Tree said. "And he's been in Nam."

"In his head he knows that. In his heart, I am the irritating city broad who has never unloaded a truck."

"Or served in Vietnam," Tree said.

On the way home he told Freddie about his first client. "Wonderful," she said in the flat voice she employed when she wasn't paying attention to him. Not that he blamed her. Freddie had not discouraged his move into detecting, as she would not discourage anything her husband decided to undertake, but she didn't encourage it, either.

"Unfortunately, he was only twelve years old."

That got her attention. "You're kidding. He was twelve?"

"Actually, he may not even have been twelve."

"What did he want you to do?"

"Find his mother."

"What did you tell him?"

"I told him he should go to the police."

"You didn't take him to the police yourself?" A hint of disapproval.

"I should have, shouldn't I?"

"A little boy so desperate to find his mom he goes to a detective. Kind of sad."

The observation came without judgmental inflection. Except he knew damn well he was being judged, and not positively.

"I should have handled it better."

"Well, hopefully he's all right. What's his name?"

"Marcello."

"That's it, Marcello?"

"After the Italian actor."

"He's named after Marcello Mastroianni?"

"Apparently."

"But you didn't get his last name."

"That's all he said," Tree said, kicking himself for not getting the kid's last name. "Like I said, I didn't handle it so well."

They crossed Blind Pass onto Captiva Island. Their house on Andy Rosse Lane like most of the newer houses in the area, was built above the garage so that in the event of a hurricane—Charley in 2004 remained fresh in everyone's mind—flood damage would be minimal. Such were the concessions you made to life in the tropics, Tree reflected. You lived in air, floating, not tethered to anything.

The house was lost in a profusion of palm trees and hedges. A sitting room with big windows showing a view of the sea dominated. A good-sized kitchen had been recently updated with de rigueur granite counters and stainless steel appliances. When they moved in, they had redone the place in bright Mediterranean tones and hung the paintings they'd collected—the oversized poster for the bad French movie Tree had written in Paris was consigned to a wall in the laundry room.

Freddie cooked turkey burgers on their Weber barbecue using real charcoal. Gas barbecues were nothing but outdoor stoves, she said. Not really barbecues at all. She had a glass of chardonnay.

After dinner they sat on the terrace overlooking the pool they never used, watching one of the spectacular sunsets tourists came from all over the world to see. Tree watched that sun in all its dying glory and decided life was not so bad.

He thought no further of twelve-year-old boys looking for their mothers.

3

A tall man with dark hair in a white linen suit waited for Tree when he arrived at the office the next
morning. Tree couldn't take his eyes off the linen suit.
It fell gracefully along the contours of his visitor's slim
torso. Linen wrinkled so easily, thought Tree, who did
not own a lot of linen—he didn't own any. How could
this guy's suit not wrinkle?

The tall man smiled when he saw Tree. The smile
was as effortless as the way he wore that linen suit.
The smile could not hide the threatening air that hung
around him like a shroud on a coffin.

"Did you know," he said in a polite voice tinged
with the luck of the Irish, "that the osprey used to be
known as a fish hawk."

Tree removed his glasses. "I read that somewhere."

"Fish hawk," the man in the linen suit said. "I like
that better than osprey. Fish hawk sounds tougher
somehow, more primal. Don't you think?"

"I'm sorry," Tree said. "I didn't get your name."

"They mate for life, you know. The fish hawks."

"I didn't know that," Tree said.

"They build nests of sticks, and then they go back
to it each year, always adding sticks. Some of these
nests, as you might imagine, grow quite large."

"What can I do for you?" Tree said.

The man's smile tightened. "Pretty busy, son?"

"I have a number of clients to do deal with this morning," Tree said in the formal voice he adopted when lying through his teeth.

"Here's something else that's interesting about the fish hawk or the osprey, if that's what you want to call it. Once the male and female have courted and come together, the male devotes himself to providing the female with fresh fish. Romantic don't you think? Making sure his wife is fed properly. Nice."

"I've learned a great deal about the osprey this morning," Tree said. "Fascinating. But maybe we should get down to business."

"Down to business," the man said. "Interesting choice of words. Yes, I suppose we should get right down to business. You and me we've got something in common, you know."

"A love of osprey?"

"Chicago, son. The second city."

"You're from Chicago?"

"As I understand you are. Where from exactly?"

"Around and about. Lincoln Park, mostly."

"Small world. I lived on Clark, a block away from the garage where the St. Valentine's Day Massacre took place."

"Is that so?"

"Of course, it's a parking lot now. But I learned a lot in Chicago, I did. The Windy City. Indeed. Well, that's pleasant enough. Old pals and all."

"You spend a lot of time here looking for people from Chicago?"

The tall man laughed. "I don't spend any time at

all. I got out of that town a long time ago. A young lady broke my heart. But isn't it the way of the world?"

Tree just looked at him. He didn't like the way this was going. He put his glasses on again, hoping they would give him a better view of his visitor. The view did not improve.

"Okay, this is the business I want to deal with this morning," the tall man said. "I require your help."

"Something to do with fish hawks?"

"With locating a certain person."

"A person. What kind of person?"

"The kind of person who makes me very angry running away like that."

"Another heartbreaker?"

"A man can only take one of those in a lifetime."

"You want me to find this person for you?"

"In a manner of speaking, yes."

"It would help to know your name," Tree said.

"My name? I didn't tell you my name?"

"I'm afraid not."

He laughed out loud. "Isn't that damnedest thing? All this talk about Chicago, I forgot. Reno, son. Reno O'Hara."

"Tree Callister."

"Yes, I know that. Mr. Tree Callister from Chicago. Tree. A funny name for a man. I hope you don't mind me saying that."

"You wouldn't be the first person who has commented on it over the years."

Reno O'Hara glanced around the room. "Tell me something, Tree."

"What's that, Reno?"

"When is the last time anyone hit you?"

Tree looked at him.

"I suspect it was in a schoolyard, right? Something like that. Or maybe at a bar when you were a young man. You know, pushing and shoving after too many drinks. Maybe over a girl. Youthful fights, they are almost always over a girl, don't you think?"

Tree did not respond.

"But I'm not talking about things like that, minor scuffles. I'm talking about really getting hit—a fist in the mouth, for example. Or someone who knows how to do it, punching you in the stomach. You really get hit, and you feel it. None of this stuff like in the movies where the hero shakes it off and then comes back and lands the punches that defeat his opponent. I'm talking about getting hit like it's a freight train running into you, like you go to the hospital, and they have to rewire your jaw or tape your ribs. Recovery takes weeks accompanied by such tremendous hurt, the doctor must prescribe powerful painkillers. You are on, like workman's compensation, although maybe a guy like you, a guy named for a tree, who is a loser and doesn't earn shit, there is no workman's compensation."

Tree was frozen in place. Reno O'Hara rewarded Tree's tense silence with an understanding smile.

"So you tell me what I need to know, and we avoid all the unpleasantness I have just discussed with you. That makes sense don't it, Tree?"

Reno was right. No one had ever hit him. Not even in school. Or during a barroom brawl. What sort of newspaperman was he, anyway, that he never got into a fist fight? Reporters in his day fought all the time; they brawled in the street, for God's sake. But somehow he had avoided all that. When he got drunk during his drinking days, he transformed into the world's nicest guy. Good old Tree. Well, right now good old Tree was in trouble, and he wasn't quite certain how to handle it.

"Look, we've still got a bit of a problem here, Reno." Tree tried his best to sound reasonable. That's what would work in a situation like this. Reason.

"What problem is that?"

"I don't know what you're talking about."

Reno's face went dark. Tree found himself being lifted off his chair and slammed against the wall. His reading glasses spun away. A framed photograph of a bikini-clad beauty catching a marlin crashed to the floor. Reno's taut face deployed in a shower of bursting stars.

"You tell her. Okay? Tell her."

"Tell who?" Tree managed to gurgle.

"She comes back, no hard feelings. Everything is A-okay again. Got that?"

"A-okay. Right."

Reno let go of him and backed away. His face no longer resembled a storm brewing. A smile played at his lips. "Where did she find you, son? What is there? Some sort of Florida Loser Club? You just call up and they send over a loser?"

"Yeah, that's it all right," Tree agreed, trying to catch his breath. "Let me give you some advice. Get away from this shit. As far as you can. You know what I can do to a guy who gets in my way. This is what I do, son. I scare myself sometimes. So make sure you don't get on my wrong side again, okay?"

"Okay."

"Just stay away from her."

And then Reno O'Hara was gone. Tree stood there. Gulping for air.